THERE'S MORE THAN ONE WAY TO SENSE A KILLER

PIPER ASHWELL PSYCHIC P.I., BOOK 16

KELLY HASHWAY

To Ayla with love

CHAPTER ONE

Not long ago, I only had to worry about myself and my adorable golden retriever, Jezebel. Then I let Detective Mitchell Brennan talk me into marrying him. We'd already been working together for quite some time since the Weltunkin PD utilizes my P.I. agency on a pretty regular basis. Mitchell and I had fallen into a routine, where he respected my need for space and I attempted to act like a normal girlfriend even though I'm anything but normal. Things were fine until my husband decided to get himself suspended from the force for threatening the chief of police on my behalf. Having Mitchell follow me around for the past two weeks and getting no break from his emotions, which come off of him in waves has wreaked havoc on my psychic abilities.

But today...today feels like Independence Day. Mitchell woke up at the crack of dawn and went to the station for his first official day back on the force. I've had a smile on my face since the moment I woke up with no one else in my bed but Jez, who was still snoring on Mitchell's pillow. My face might actually be cramping from smiling so much as I count the twenty-three steps from my office to Marcia's Nook to get coffee and breakfast for Dad and me. As soon as the bell above the door announces me, Marcia looks up from the register in the café where she's ringing up a customer. She cocks her head at me and finishes her transaction. Once the woman takes her bag and leaves, I step up to the counter.

"You look particularly happy this morning," Marcia says.

"Mitchell went back to work today." I shouldn't sound so happy to get rid of my husband. I know. But I also see why wives complain so much when their husbands retire. Those poor women. Mitchell was like a lost soul being at home all the time. He's not a reader like I am, and unless I'm curled up on the couch with him, the man has trouble sitting still.

Marcia chuckles and bobs her head. "I see. He was driving you crazy, wasn't he?"

"Is it that obvious?"

She pours me an extra-large toasted almond coffee, my usual. "Well, I did notice you've bought more books in the past two weeks than usual, and for you that's saying something. I assumed you were reading to avoid Mitchell."

"I swear he had no clue what to do with himself. Even

Jez was getting annoyed with him, and Mitchell has always been her favorite person." I used to joke that Jez was Mitchell's girlfriend. I think she believes that's true, anyway. Before Mitchell and I got married, Jezebel would get so sad every time he left my apartment. "She's been exhausted because he takes her on so many runs with him."

"Mitchell was already in great shape. How much more running could he do?" Marcia asks, capping my coffee and pouring Dad's.

It's no secret Mitchell is extremely good-looking. Women eye him up all the time, and the extra workouts have toned him even more. Luckily for me, ever since Mitchell and I got together, he makes sure other women know he's not available. The man has his faults, but loyalty is not one of them. I try not to say it to his face because his ego is the size of a blimp, but I definitely lucked out with him. He's never once doubted my abilities, and from the very first case we worked on together, he's learned ways to make it easier for me to not only have visions but recover from them. My strengths lie in psychometry, reading the energy off objects to see the past, present, and sometimes future. The problem is that when I experience visions from the victim's viewpoint, I take on the victim's symptoms. It's landed me in the hospital on numerous occasions. I used to think the effects were just phantom injuries, not really there but my mind believed they were real. My most recent trip to the emergency room helped me see that I can absolutely be physically affected by my visions as well. That part scares me, and it is only going to make Mitchell want to be even more careful every time I try to read an object and spark a vision.

"Did I lose you?" Marcia asks, waving a hand in front of me.

"Sorry, I zoned out."

"That's your defense mechanism when you don't want to talk about something. So tell me what I can get you to go with the coffees." Marcia is my best friend, after Mitchell. She's really my only friend other than Mitchell. It's hard for me to get close to people, but Marcia understands me, and she keeps me caffeinated. She also owns this bookstore and puts aside all the new releases she thinks I'll like.

"Anything recently come out of the oven?" I ask, sipping my coffee.

She holds up a finger. "I could use some taste testers." Marcia knows Mitchell, Dad, and I love taste testing for her. "I made some pecan pie muffins."

"I don't think I've ever tried one before."

"It's like a cross between pie and a muffin, so the inside is actually gooey. Are you up for being my guinea pig?"

"Of course. That sounds delicious."

She disappears inside the kitchen and returns with a tray of mammoth muffins. She boxes up three.

"Oh, I don't think Mitchell will be joining Dad and me this morning." I pause. "On second thought, I'll eat his." I have a wickedly fast metabolism that leaves me bonier than most people despite how much I eat.

Marcia laughs and juts her chin toward the door. The bell rings as someone enters.

"No. Don't even tell me," I say.

"Good morning, Detective," Marcia says with a smile.

I don't turn around. Instead, I count Mitchell's footsteps as they sound across the floor. When he reaches me, he loops his arm around my waist.

"Good morning." He places a kiss on the side of my head.

Marcia is stifling a laugh.

One morning. That's all I wanted. One morning to myself.

"Ooh, what are those?" Mitchell asks, looking into the box as Marcia closes the lid.

"Pecan pie muffins. You're just in time, too. Piper hasn't paid yet."

Mitchell whips out his wallet. "Did you find a new book?" he asks me. "You've really been flying through them lately."

So he did notice my excessive reading.

Marcia reaches under the counter. "I put one aside for you. It's a new release that sounds right up your alley, Piper." She puts it on top of the pastry box.

"Thanks, Marcia."

Mitchell hands Marcia a fifty. "Piper, we need to run. We've got a case."

Marcia rings up the order and tries to give Mitchell his change, but he grabs our food and my book and hurries me out the door. "No time. You hang on to that," he tells Marcia. He's always giving her insanely large tips. He told me she deserves them because she works so hard and runs this place practically all on her own, but I know it's also because Marcia is such a good friend to us.

She shakes her head at Mitchell as we leave.

"Is there really a case?" I ask him, not sure if he just said that to get Marcia to keep his change.

"Yes. I'm not a liar, Piper."

"I know, but I also know you'll do just about anything to tip Marcia."

"True, but there is a case, and I even brought something for you to read."

He means "read" as in with my psychometry abilities. I smile at him. He knows case files don't do much for me. I need objects that belong to the victim. It's the quickest way for me to solve a case. "You're learning, Detective."

With a smile on his face, he opens the door of my office for me. He used to hate when I called him Detective, but now that we're married, he thinks it's flirting. Maybe it is.

"Morning, you two," Dad says, looking up at us from his oversized desk. Don't even get me started on that subject. He joined my P.I. agency after retiring from the WPD and bought a desk twice the size of mine. It's humiliating. He claims he didn't realize it would be that big, but I can tell he loves it.

"Hey, Dad," Mitchell says. He looks at the coffees in my hands. "Wait, where's my coffee?"

"I didn't know you were coming into the office," I say, handing Dad his before taking a seat at my desk.

Mitchell slumps down in the seat across from me just as Jax, Marcia's employee and delivery guy, walks in. "Good morning. Detective Brennan, I have your coffee for you. I've been instructed not to accept payment or a tip since you left Marcia so much money a few minutes ago. She's tipping me from that."

"Ha-ha," I say to Mitchell. I enjoy the ways Marcia tries to get back at Mitchell for over tipping.

"Thank you, Jax," Mitchell says, taking the coffee from him.

Jax immediately backs up and hurries out before Mitchell can even attempt to grab his wallet and tip him anyway.

"So, what's the case?" I ask, opening the pastry box and handing Dad a muffin before grabbing one myself.

Dad takes a big bite. "Wow! What are these? They're amazing."

"Pecan pie muffins," I say before taking a bite myself. He's right. They're phenomenal. I text Marcia to let her know and then devour the rest of my muffin. Dad and Mitchell do the same, and the office is silent for several minutes while we enjoy our food heaven.

Once we're finished, Mitchell opens the case file. "The victim is twenty-three-year-old Isabelle DiMarco. She's a former gymnast. At sixteen, she was at the height of her career. But then she was involved in a car accident. She got hit by a tractor trailer. It's a wonder she even survived. Apparently, the driver did everything he could to try to avoid her. Luckily, the accident occurred when the truck was driving around a bend at a slow speed. Still, Isabelle suffered severe head trauma." Mitchell consults the file in his hands. "What happened to her is called traumatic optic neuropathy. It basically means the optic nerve was injured beyond repair, resulting in irreversible vision loss. Once she recovered from the other injuries incurred during the accident, she returned to her former gym as a coach to help train her younger sister, Valentina."

"She coached blind?" Dad asks, showing just how impressed he is by that.

"Yeah, and she was apparently really good at it, too," Mitchell says.

"How did she die?" I ask since he's only told us about Isabelle's accident when she was sixteen. It's been seven years since that happened. And there's no way any lingering injuries caused her death. There wouldn't be a case for us to solve if that was what happened.

"She was found murdered in her home. Cause of death was blunt force trauma to her head." Mitchell hands a paper to Dad, and I'm sure it contains photographs from the crime scene.

Dad looks over the paper before giving me a questioning look. I hate seeing dead bodies. And honestly, if there is a clue in any of the crime scene photos, Dad and Mitchell are just as capable of seeing it as I am.

I discreetly shake my head. I don't want to see the pictures yet. If I get stumped on the case, I'll look at them, but for now, I'll pass.

"Did you find the murder weapon?" I ask.

"No. We're not even sure what it was yet."

This is where I come in. "You said you brought something for me to read." I hold out my hand.

Mitchell reaches into his pants pocket and pulls out an evidence bag. He knows not to touch objects before I read them. I need to sense Isabelle's energy on it, not Mitchell's. "Her parents said this was her most prized possession." Mitchell holds up the bag so I can see the gold medal it contains. "Isabelle won this the night she was in the car accident that took her eyesight. Her parents said she kissed the medal every night before bed."

"That's sad," Dad says. "The accident ended what would have been an amazing future in gymnastics. She was on top of the competition when it happened."

It definitely is sad, but it also makes the medal the perfect object for me to read. "Good job, Mitchell." I reach for the medal. Isabelle's energy is all over it, beckoning me to read the object.

Mitchell hesitates. "Piper, after what happened last time, I'm not sure this is a good idea. Maybe you should try to get a sense of Isabelle without coming into physical contact with this."

I cock my head at him. "You want me to have a vision without touching the medal? Did you forget how psychometry works?"

"No. I don't think you should have a vision at all. You just need to get a sense of Isabelle's energy, right?"

That's pointless, and we both know it. "And do what with it?" I ask, choosing not to come out and tell him how idiotic his plan is.

Mitchell shrugs and has the decency to avoid my gaze. "Maybe you'll be able to tell if she was scared or thought someone was watching her."

"Dad, help me out here," I say, keeping my eyes locked on Mitchell. "Tell Mitchell I have to have a vision. Tiptoeing around this isn't going to help at all."

Dad clears his throat. "Pumpkin, I think I'm with Mitchell on this one."

I lean back in my chair and cross my arms. "Unbelievable. Why did you bring this case to me if you don't want my help? Maybe you two should solve it, and I'll take my new book home to read."

Dad's phone rings. "It's your mother. I'm going to take this outside and let you two hash this out." He gets up and walks out of the office.

"Piper, please be reasonable," Mitchell starts, but I hold up a hand to stop him.

"Reasonable is thinking the psychic will use her

psychic abilities to solve the murder. If one of us is being unreasonable, it's you." Mitchell likes to be part of my process by holding my left hand and grounding me during my visions. Maybe I'm playing dirty by asking him for his help, but I don't see another option. "Keep me grounded. You've pulled me out of visions before. I trust you to do the same for me now."

He shakes his head. "I can't believe you're trying that trick on me."

"It's not a trick. We're a team, aren't we?" I hold up my left hand so he can see my wedding ring. "Isn't that what this means?"

He reaches forward and laces his fingers through mine. "I will rip that medal out of your hand the second anything looks off to me."

"Deal." It's the best I can hope for with him.

With his free hand, he unzips the bag and dumps the medal onto my desk.

I take several deep breaths and focus on the energy I can already feel rolling off the object. Mitchell squeezes my left hand, signaling he's here for me. I close my eyes as my fingers wrap around the medal.

Isabelle is singing along to her music as she drives. Then she's jolted to the left, her head connecting with the window.

Mitchell yanks the medal from my hand. "Sorry, but you jerked your head. I thought something bad was happening."

"It was. I saw the car accident." I try to open my eyes, but it's not working. I rub them with the heels of my hands and try again, but I get the same result. "I can't open my eyes." My voice comes out squeaky, reflecting my fear.

I hear Mitchell's footsteps as he walks around my desk to me and takes my face in his hands. "Piper, your eyes are open."

What? No. That can't be. All I see is black. Oh my God. "Mitchell." This time my voice cracks. "I can't see. I think I'm blind."

CHAPTER TWO

Mitchell uses his fingers to open my eyelids. "You can't see anything?"

"No. It's all black."

"What happened in the vision?"

"I saw the accident from when Isabelle was sixteen."

Mitchell's hand falls from my face. "The one that blinded Isabelle." He groans, and even though I can't see him, I know he's stood up. "This is my fault. I'm such an idiot for bringing you this medal to read. Isabelle was wearing it during the accident."

Had I known that, I might not have tried to read it. It makes perfect sense that I saw the accident.

The door to the office creaks open. "Sorry about that," Dad says. "Your mother wanted to see if I could meet her for lunch today."

"Dad—" Mitchell stops abruptly, and the next thing I

know I feel his energy invading my space. He must be squatting down beside me again.

"What happened?" Dad asks, worry in his voice. "Piper?"

"I'm okay, Dad. I just can't see anything."

Footsteps stomp across the floor as Dad moves toward me. "What is she talking about, Mitchell?"

"It's not his fault," I say.

"Yes, it is." Mitchell cups my face. "Piper, I'm so sorry. I should have known..."

"Should have known what?" Dad yells. "Someone tell me what happened."

Mitchell lets go of me, and I hear the crinkling of the plastic bag as he places the medal back inside it. "She read the medal."

Dad's sharp intake of air is deafening. Or maybe it's just that my other senses are working overtime to compensate for my lack of sight. "She's blind because that's what happened to Isabelle."

"Yeah," I say. "The question is will I stay this way, or will it wear off like the effects of my visions usually do?"

"We need to take you to the hospital," Mitchell says. "Nurse Vera will check you out."

Nurse Vera is the only one I like at the hospital. I trust her. "Okay." I can't see their reactions, but I'd bet money they're both staring at me with wide eyes. I've never willingly gone to the hospital before, but I need to know if this blindness is real or not. I stand up, and Mitchell wraps his arm around me.

"Do you want me to carry you?" he asks.

"There's nothing wrong with my legs." I take one step away from him, so his arm drops from my waist.

"Yeah, but you can't see."

I picture the office in my head. Luckily, I can still do that. My mind's eye hasn't been affected by this blindness, and I'm thankful for that much. I open up my senses, searching for the energy each object around me contains. I start moving toward the door.

"Well, look at that," Dad says.

Mitchell's energy is annoyingly close to me, so I know he's hovering, staying within a pinky finger's reach of me. "The door is—"

"I know," I tell him. "Mitchell, I've got this." I'm not going to sprint through any mazes anytime soon, but moving at a slow pace like this is totally doable thanks to my senses. I reach for the door handle and pull.

"I'll stay here and see what I can find out about Isabelle DiMarco," Dad says. "I want an update as soon as you have one, Mitchell."

"You got it." Mitchell loops my arm through his once we're outside.

"Mitchell, I'm fine. Seriously—"

"I know." He stops walking judging by the gentle tug backward on my arm, so I stop as well. "Piper, you're incredible. Anyone else would be freaking out in your position right now, but not only are you remaining calm, but you're getting around fine. I'm not holding on to you because I think you need my help. I'm doing it because I'm in awe of you."

"Thank you. Now let's get to the hospital and figure out what this is so we can get to work on the case."

Mitchell gets the car door for me, and I don't protest because he'd do that even if I wasn't blind. The ride to the hospital is interesting. I can hear every sound outside. The birds, the wind, other cars on the road, even the faint squeak of Mitchell's brakes. "You should get new brakes," I say as we walk inside the hospital.

Mitchell's energy shifts.

"You're furrowing your brow, aren't you?"

"How did you know? Has your vision returned?"

"Stop waving your hand in front of my face," I say.

"You can see."

"No, I can sense your energy, and I know you well enough to know what those subtle shifts in your energy mean."

"Like the gestures associated with them?" he asks.

I bob my head.

"Incredible." He kisses my forehead. "Come on. The elevator is this way."

"I know."

Mitchell takes my left hand in his despite my declaration. I let him have this one because I don't want to constantly argue with him. Also, if I do accidentally walk into something here at the hospital, I might wind up as a patient and have to sneak out for the umpteenth time. I really just want to see Vera in private, get my diagnosis, and leave.

Being in enclosed spaces with people is never a comfortable experience for me, and with my heightened senses, it's particularly bad. There are four other people in the elevator with Mitchell and me. Each one has a different energy. One is really upset. Another is annoyed. The person closest to me is worried. And the fourth person seems to be here with intentions to propose. That's an odd one. I move closer to Mitchell, and he positions me between him and the elevator wall, trying to shield me from the others.

"You okay?" he asks me.

"I will be once we get out of here."

He wraps his arms around me, and I feel the steady rise and fall of his chest. He's trying to calm himself so his energy will soothe me. It's actually working, too. I rest my head against his chest, but that makes his heartbeat quicken.

"Sorry," he says, noticing the change in himself. "You have that effect on me."

I tilt my head up to him, wishing I could see his beautiful green eyes.

"You miss seeing my handsome face, don't you?" he teases.

I laugh, and I realize that was his intention. He's

keeping my focus off the others in the elevator. I hear the ding, announcing our arrival on Vera's floor, and Mitchell leads me out.

"Thank you," I say.

"Happy to help. I see Vera." He brings me to her.

"Oh, boy. I see trouble has arrived. What can I do for you two?" Vera asks us.

"Can we speak privately?" Mitchell asks her.

I pick up on her suspicion. She thinks we're up to something. "I had an unforeseen side-effect to a vision that I need to discuss with you," I tell her.

"Oh. Okay. This room here is empty."

Mitchell leads me into the room.

"Hold on." The click of the door tells me Vera's making sure no one overhears us. "Piper, what's wrong with your eyesight?"

"Everything." I reach for the bed and sit down. "I sort of read an object belonging to a woman who went blind, and well, now I can't see a thing."

Another soft click and a light is being shone in my eye.

"I can see that," I say.

"It's not uncommon for blind people to be able to see light. Tell me how this woman lost her vision."

Mitchell fills Vera in on the car accident.

"I see. So it was the trauma to the head that caused it. Piper, do you have sensitivity to your head?"

"No, none."

"Okay, that's good. I'd like to run some tests, but I'm willing to bet this is a phantom symptom."

"Nurse Vera, can we keep this strictly between us? We don't want to have Piper admitted. We have a case to get back to."

"You plan to work a case while you can't see?" she asks.

"My other senses are perfectly fine. Actually, they're more acute than usual."

She's quiet for a moment. "Tell you what. Let me run some tests, and then, depending on the results, we'll figure out if Piper would be better off staying here or at home resting until her vision returns."

"Thank you," Mitchell says.

Vera's tests involve putting drops in my eyes that allow her to see everything inside using a light. She's very thorough, and my patience is running thin by the time she tells me she's finished.

"Well, there's no swelling or abnormalities of any kind," Vera says.

"Then this is merely an effect of the vision. It should go away," I say.

"As far as I can tell, yes," Nurse Vera says. "But, Piper, that doesn't mean you shouldn't take this seriously. Without the use of your sight, you're extremely vulnerable."

"You'd be surprised by how well she's adapting," Mitchell says.

I get off the bed and reach out with my senses to get the layout of the room. Then I walk over to the television on the wall and turn it on.

"How did you do that?" Nurse Vera asks.

"Easy. I find the energy in the room." I laugh. "I kind of feel like a bat. You know the way they use echolocation to find things in the dark? What I'm doing is similar, except I'm sensing energy instead of using sound."

"You're like Bat Woman," Mitchell says.

"If you're picturing me in some form-fitting hero getup, you can knock it off right now," I say.

Vera laughs. "You two are something. Listen, Piper, I know you don't like to be told you can't do something, so I'm just going to tell you to be careful. And if your vision hasn't returned in forty-eight hours, you should come back to see me."

"Thank you, Nurse Vera. I'll take good care of her," Mitchell says.

"I have no doubt you will, but I know Piper. She's a sneaky one. No disappearing acts. Stick with your husband."

"That's the best prescription I've ever heard," Mitchell says.

I roll my eyes.

We say goodbye to Nurse Vera and exit the hospital.

"Where do you want to start?" Mitchell asks once we're on the road.

"I want to see the crime scene." I pause at my poor choice of words. "You know what I mean."

"Isabelle lives in a detached garage on her parents' property. They converted it to an apartment for her after she turned eighteen."

I'm guessing she wanted some independence but also understood her limitations. It's a good compromise. She was still close to her parents if she needed help, but she had her privacy as well.

"Piper, do you think there's a reason why seeing Isabelle in the vision caused you to take on her blindness?"

I know he's been wondering this from the start. "You think I connected to something personal. She wasn't psychic if that's what you're thinking." It's not a bad guess, though.

"It's just that I've never seen you connect to a victim so much after only one vision."

"I can't explain it. Maybe my senses are trying to tell me I need to step into Isabelle's shoes to figure out who killed her. We know losing my vision is heightening my other senses. It could be that's what I need to solve this case."

"So you don't think you'll regain your eyesight until the case is over?"

"Eyes on the road, Detective," I reprimand. "I could feel your gaze on me."

He lets out a deep breath. "You're almost scary good at being blind."

I lace my fingers together in my lap. "I don't like not being able to see. It forces me to reach out with my senses, and I've spent my entire life trying to keep other people's energy away from me."

"Nurse Vera said this is only temporary, so let's solve this case and show your senses that they don't need to keep your eyesight from you any longer." Mitchell parks the car and walks around to get my door. "Since you don't like reaching out with your senses, why don't you let me help you get around?"

"Okay." I'm sure his expression is one of shock. He's right, though. If I'm constantly reaching out with my senses, I'll exhaust myself or overwhelm myself. I don't want to do either. I loop my arm through his.

"There are three steps up to the front door. We're coming up on the first one." He slows down, and I step up, missing on my first try.

"You go first. I want to use the sound to judge my distance."

"Bat Woman," Mitchell says.

"Yeah, kind of. I'm still not wearing a costume."

"Not even for Halloween?"

I better have my eyesight back well before Halloween. I roll my eyes. "Move, Detective. We don't have all day."

He steps up, and I use the sound to judge where I am in comparison. I make it up the steps and smile. Mitchell rings the doorbell.

A few moments later, a woman says, "Can I help

you?" Her voice is shaky, like she's been crying. This must be Mrs. DiMarco.

"Mrs. DiMarco?" Mitchell asks. I assume she nods because he continues. "I'm Detective Brennan with the Weltunkin Police Department, and this is my partner, Piper Ashwell. We're investigating your daughter's death. May we come inside and speak to you?"

"Of course. Please come in."

Mitchell leads me into the house. The energy in here is heavy with grief.

"We're very sorry for your loss," I say.

"Is she...I mean, are you blind?" From living with Isabelle, Mrs. DiMarco probably realized it would be in poor taste to talk about me when she can ask me directly.

"Temporarily," I say. Mitchell tugs on my arm, and I realize we're standing in front of a couch. I lower myself, using my left hand as a guide. "Mrs. DiMarco, I'm a psychic P.I. I specialize in something called psychometry, which is reading the energy off objects. I read your daughter's gymnastics medal, the one she was wearing—"

"When she had the car accident," Mrs. DiMarco finishes for me.

"Yes. I saw what happened, and as a result, I found myself temporarily blind."

"That's horrible."

At least she's not calling me a fraud and claiming I'm mocking her deceased daughter. "There's nothing physically wrong with my eyes. I think I'm just channeling Isabelle."

"What does that mean exactly? Do you talk to spirits?"

"No. I'm not a medium. But I can use my abilities to hopefully find out what happened to your daughter."

"Piper and I would like to look around the crime scene, but we wanted to ask you a few questions first." The soft squeal of cardboard on metal tells me Mitchell has his notepad out, ready to jot down anything important that Mrs. DiMarco might tell us.

She swallows so hard I hear it.

"I know this is difficult, but anything you remember would help us," I say.

"I saw Isabelle Saturday night after she returned from the gym. Valentina, my other daughter, drives her. They'd gotten into an argument." Her voice quivers. She can't possibly think Valentina harmed Isabelle, can she?

CHAPTER THREE

Mrs. DiMarco's energy shifts. She's very guarded right now, like she's holding back. I can't tell if she thinks Valentina is the killer or if she's ashamed of something.

"Did they fight often?" Mitchell asks.

"Isabelle had a tendency to push Valentina in her training. I think Isabelle was trying to fulfill her own dreams through her sister." Mrs. DiMarco sniffles. "At first, Valentina was okay with it because she felt awful for her sister, but over the years, it wore on Valentina, and they started arguing about it."

"Do you know what they argued about Saturday night?" Mitchell asks.

"Nothing out of the ordinary. Valentina was having a tough time with a new routine on the balance beam. Isabelle said she wasn't trying hard enough, and Valentina told her she'd like to see her do better." Mrs. DiMarco starts sobbing. "Then Isabelle told Valentina she was never going to get as many trophies as she won if she didn't start acting like a true competitor."

Trophies.

"The trophies are important," I tell Mitchell. Sometimes my senses throw something out at me as a truth. It's more helpful when it's a clear message, but it can be vague, like right now, leaving me to figure out the meaning.

"What do you mean?" Mrs. DiMarco asks.

"I'm not sure yet. Was Valentina training for a specific competition?"

"Yes. It's the same one..." She stops talking abruptly.

"The same one Isabelle took first place in the night of her car accident," I say.

"Yes." The word is barely audible.

First Isabelle has the accident on the night of that competition, and now she's murdered while training her younger sister to compete in it. That can't be a coincidence.

"Was Saturday night the last time you saw Isabelle?" Mitchell asks. He means saw her alive. Mrs. DiMarco most likely found her daughter dead in the morning.

She doesn't verbally respond, so I assume she nods.

"Okay, well, we're going to check out Isabelle's apartment. Here is my card. If you think of anything at all, please don't hesitate to call me."

I stand up, and Mitchell immediately wraps my arm around his.

"Ms. Ashwell," Mrs. DiMarco says. "I'm sorry this happened to you. Isabelle wouldn't have wanted this. She wanted the best for everyone. She pushed Valentina because she believed in her. I can't imagine anyone wanting to harm her."

Twice.

"What?" I say, not meaning to voice my confusion aloud.

"I said I can't imagine anyone wanting to harm her," Mrs. DiMarco repeats, assuming I was speaking to her.

Twice.

Interesting. I don't tell Mitchell what my senses told me until we're alone on our way to Isabelle's apartment.

"What was that?" he asks.

"My senses said someone tried to harm Isabelle twice."

"When was the other time?"

"I'm not sure."

"Should we play the game?" Mitchell asks. The game is something we use on most cases. I clear my mind, and Mitchell asks me questions I already know the answers to. Once I get into a meditative state, he starts directing his questions toward the case, and an answer or two will come to me as a truth. It usually doesn't produce much because I get shocked out of the meditative state by my own responses. It's good for getting leads, though.

I stop walking and bob my head. Then I take several

deep breaths to center myself. When I'm ready, I give Mitchell's arm a squeeze since I'm still holding on to him.

"What's your father's name?" he begins.

"Thomas."

"Who is our landlord?"

"Theodore Hall."

"What kind of car do you drive?"

"A Mazda 6."

"Has someone tried to hurt Isabelle DiMarco before?"

"Yes."

"When?"

"Seven years ago." The answer jolts me out of the game. "That has to mean the car accident, right?"

"That would mean it wasn't an accident," Mitchell says. "I can look into it, but I'm almost certain there was no mention of foul play. Car accidents happen all the time."

"I guess it could mean something else. Maybe someone tried to hurt her before the competition to keep her from winning."

"Let's go check out the crime scene. If you don't get anything concrete, I think we need to visit the gym and find out more about this competition."

His plan is solid and exactly what I was thinking. Mitchell opens the door to the apartment. "There's no step this time. You can walk right inside."

I do. I let go of Mitchell, allowing myself to focus on Isabelle's energy in the apartment.

"It's a studio," Mitchell says.

"Don't tell me. I want to see what I sense first."

"Okay. Let me know if you want me to help you walk around the room."

I need to try it on my own. I reach out with my right hand. One mystery I've never solved about my own abilities is why I need to use my right hand to read energy. It's just something I've come to accept. My hand touches a piece of furniture and the television sitting on top of it. I continue and reach a shelf. There's a lot of energy coming from it.

I feel the objects on it. "Trophies," I say.

"Yes." Mitchell is at my side.

"My senses said the trophies were important, but the competition that seems to be key gives out medals."

"You're right. But maybe it's the fact that Isabelle won so many competitions. It could have caused animosity with the other competitors."

Yes. "That's true," I say. "My senses confirmed it."

I know he's smiling. Mitchell's mother was psychic, and he's always wished he had some psychic abilities himself. Still, he doesn't tell anyone about his mother, mostly because she foresaw her own death and didn't try to stop it because she thought doing so would harm Mitchell and his younger brother, Nick. Mom knows about Mitchell's mother, though. I told her, and Mitchell knows I shared that secret with her. He's okay with it because my mom is like his second mother, and he trusts her.

I pick up the nearest trophy. Even though I can't see, I still close my eyes before trying to spark a vision. It's just second nature to do so.

Isabelle is standing on the podium, smiling from ear to ear. Beside her in the second-place spot is a blonde girl with curly hair. She glares at Isabelle. And on the opposite side in the third-place position is a redhead who appears equally upset with Isabelle.

"Her competitors don't seem to have liked her much at all," I say.

"You saw them?"

"Yeah, my mind's eye is still functioning fine. I saw the girls who came in second and third to Isabelle."

"What did they look like?" Mitchell asks.

"One had curly blonde hair, and the other was a redhead. We should look up that competition and find out who those girls are." My visions always show me things that are important to the case I'm working on, which means I saw those girls for a reason.

"Okay, I'm making a note. We can do that as soon as we finish up here."

"Better yet, call my dad." He's a whiz with research.

"On it." I hear Mitchell dialing as I place the trophy back on the shelf. "Dad, it's Mitchell." He pauses, and I can feel his embarrassment. "Right, no other male calls you that. Anyway, um, Piper and I need you to look into..." He pauses again. "Piper, let me see that trophy."

I reach for it again and hand it to Mitchell.

"Okay, it's the regional competition." He rattles off the year it took place. "We need to know the names of the girls who came in second and third place to Isabelle. I'm not sure of the event. Piper, do you know what event it was for?" he asks me.

"No, sorry. I couldn't tell from my vision."

"I guess just get us a list of all the winners. Piper should be able to—" He stops abruptly.

I can look at a list of names, and anyone important to the case will pop out at me, their name appearing bigger and bolder than the rest, but I can't exactly do that when I can't see.

"We'll figure it out from there," Mitchell says.

"Sorry," I say once he ends the call.

"Don't apologize. This isn't your fault at all." He rubs his hand up and down my arm. "I was hoping you having another vision of Isabelle might reverse the effects of the previous vision."

"You're quite the optimist."

"Hey, I wouldn't have stood a chance with you if I wasn't." Mitchell claims he knew from the start that we were meant to be together. It took a lot of pushing on his end to get me to admit he was right.

"Okay, tell me about this apartment. Describe it to me."

"There's a couch in front of the television you found. The TV stand is full of DVDs. I'm pretty sure they're all old gymnastics competitions. There's a small kitchen area in the left corner. No stove, though. Only a microwave, refrigerator, and a few cabinets. The back wall has a murphy bed, which is up at the moment."

"It's up? Meaning Isabelle was killed Saturday night and never slept in the bed."

"Correct. According to the coroner, she was killed sometime shortly after midnight, which I suppose makes it Sunday morning if we're being technical."

"And we know both Mrs. DiMarco and Valentina saw Isabelle Saturday night after Isabelle came home from the gym."

"Did you get the feeling Mrs. DiMarco questioned Valentina?" Mitchell asks.

"At first, yes, but now I think it was actually more fear of *us* questioning Valentina."

"I want to look for photo albums," Mitchell says.

"Does anyone keep those anymore?" I ask.

"Not typically, but seven years ago, maybe."

"You're thinking Isabelle had photographs of her on the winner's podium, and Valentina might be able to identify the two girls I saw in my vision."

"You got it. It gives us a reason to talk to her that won't make her suspicious, too."

"Good thinking." I turn around even though it doesn't make any difference since I can't see the apartment. "Anything else in here I should know about?"

"There's a dresser next to the murphy bed. Do you want any other belongings to read?"

What he means is reading the medal again could be dangerous. The first time I read the medal, I didn't feel the head trauma Isabelle suffered in the car accident. We don't know if I'll be that lucky the second time around. Not that losing my eyesight is really lucky.

I reach out with my right hand, trying to see if anything calls to my senses. I'm drawn back to the shelf with the trophies. I'm not surprised since my senses have already clued me in that they're important.

"What is it?" Mitchell asks.

"I don't know." I allow my hand to be guided to a spot in the center of the shelf. I reach for what I assume will be a trophy, but I come up empty. "What's over here?" I ask.

Mitchell is at my side again. "Nothing. The spot is empty."

I reach forward and place my palm flat against the shelf. "It wasn't empty. Or it shouldn't be. Something was moved. Taken from here."

"A trophy?" he asks.

"I would assume so."

"Why would a trophy be missing?" Mitchell asks.

Murder weapon.

I inhale sharply. "It's the murder weapon, Mitchell. That's what caused the blunt force trauma to Isabelle's head. She was beaten to death with one of her own trophies."

"Are you sure?"

"Not one hundred percent, but I'd still bet money on it."

"Is it just me or are your senses cluing you in on more than usual?" he asks.

"They are."

"Hmm." He taps his foot, and I count the taps. Five. Then he says, "I guess there's more than one way to sense a killer."

I should have seen that coming. No pun intended. I roll my eyes. "I'm blind, and you can't even have enough pity on me to not come up with one of your stupid sayings."

"It's a gift."

"It's something, but not a gift."

He laughs, and it sounds like he's bending down.

"What are you doing?" I ask.

"There's a basket down here. I want to see what's inside it." Something slides across the bottom of the shelf. "Well, it's not a photo album, but it might be just as good." His voice gets closer as he talks, so I know he's standing again. "It's a newspaper article, and there's a picture of Isabelle with two other girls, one blonde and the other a redhead."

"Let's bring it to Valentina and see if she can identify them and maybe tell us what was on this shelf here." I motion to where I think the spot is.

Mitchell takes my arm and loops it through his. We head back to the main house. Mrs. DiMarco doesn't answer the door this time. A man does.

"You must be the detectives my wife told me about," he says. "I'm Richard DiMarco. Constance said you were looking around Isabelle's apartment."

"Yes, we were hoping to speak to Valentina. Is she home?" Mitchell asks.

"Why do you need to speak with my daughter?" Mr. DiMarco's tone is suddenly defensive.

"We're hoping she can tell us about the girls Isabelle competed against," I say, trying to put him at ease.

"These girls in particular," Mitchell says.

"I'm afraid Valentina was only ten when that photo was taken. I'm not sure she'd remember them. My wife might, though. Come in."

Mitchell walks inside first and then helps guide me. "Mr. DiMarco, when did you last see Isabelle?"

"Saturday morning before she left for the gym. I'm afraid I was already asleep when she got home. I suffer from migraines. I had one Saturday afternoon that really took a toll on me. I was in bed by six o'clock."

I can relate to migraines. My visions can bring on awful headaches that leave me incapable of doing anything but sleeping. "I'm sorry to hear that. I know how awful migraines can be."

Mitchell is leading me through the house, but when we reach the stairs, he says, "Maybe we should ask Valentina to come downstairs."

"No." I want to see her room. "I can manage."

"Oh, that's right. My wife mentioned the issue with your eyesight. I have to admit I've never believed in psychics, but Constance is very spiritual."

I reach for the railing and use it to help me up the steps. "I have to say what's happened has given me a great deal of respect for anyone who deals with vision loss. I can't imagine life was easy for Isabelle after her accident."

"It took her a while to come to terms with her career being over."

"Dad?" a young girl says. "What's going on?"

"These detectives would like to speak with you about the girls Isabelle used to compete with," he tells her.

"Could we maybe go to your room?" I ask her. "I'd like to sit down if you don't mind."

"She's blind," Mr. DiMarco whispers to Valentina.

"What are the odds of a blind woman investigating Isabelle's death?" she says.

We walk into her room, and I'm immediately drawn to Isabelle's energy. "You have something of Isabelle's," I say.

Everyone gets quiet.

"Something in here is hers." I move forward, letting my senses guide me. My hand finds what I'm searching for. A trophy. "This is—"

"Isabelle's. Yes," Valentina says.

But something else overwhelms me. Anger. Rage. "This is the murder weapon."

CHAPTER FOUR

"What?" Mitchell asks.

"Valentina, why do you have Isabelle's trophy?" her father asks.

"What's going on?" Mrs. DiMarco asks. She must have heard us and come to see why we're back in the main house.

"Valentina, you took this from Isabelle's apartment," I say.

"Why is the murder weapon in your room?" Mitchell asks Valentina.

"Hold on," Mr. DiMarco says. "Are you accusing my daughter of something, because if you are, I want a lawyer present before she says anything."

There's only one way to find out if Valentina killed her sister. I need to read this trophy. I tune out the others in the room and focus on the energy coming from the trophy that led me to figure out it's the murder weapon.

The killer stalks slowly toward the couch where Isabelle is asleep, the movements careful and concise. No sound is being made, the footsteps are so light. The television is on with a DVD of a gymnastics meet.

The killer pauses, consumed by rage.

The trophy is ripped from my hand.

Someone is screaming.

"Piper." Mitchell wraps one arm around me, which means the trophy must be in his other hand. "What happened?"

"That's what I want to know," Mr. DiMarco yells.

"Was she going to hit me?" Valentina asks.

"No." Mitchell's voice is firm and full of authority. "Everyone needs to calm down and be quiet. Piper had a psychic vision. I'm guessing it was of Isabelle's murderer."

The sharp intake of breath by Mrs. DiMarco is followed by a thud on the floor. She must have fainted.

"Constance," Mr. DiMarco says. "We need an ambulance. Call an ambulance!"

The energy in the room is all-consuming, and I realize Mitchell is holding me up, supporting nearly all my weight.

"I'll call one," Mitchell says. "No one move." He helps me out of the room. "Piper, can you stand on your own for a second?"

I bob my head and use the wall in the hallway for

support. Mitchell slowly eases his arm from me until he's satisfied I'm okay. A moment later, he's speaking into his phone. "Wallace, I need an ambulance at the DiMarco residence. Mrs. DiMarco just fainted."

Officer Wallace is one of my favorites at the Weltunkin PD. He has a K9 partner, Harry, who actually works in a very similar way to how I do. Officer Wallace will be the first to admit he doesn't understand what I do, but that doesn't stop him from believing in it either. I appreciate that, especially since there's a detective at the WPD who is a firm nonbeliever and tries to rationalize everything I come across psychically with some other explanation that makes sense to her. I have a lot of respect for Detective Shannon O'Reilly—after all, she took a bullet for me on our last case together—but working with her can be trying at times. Needless to say, I'm glad Officer Wallace is the one who answered Mitchell's call.

"Piper, hang tight for a moment," Mitchell says, and I know he plans to go check on Mrs. DiMarco and let the family know an ambulance is on the way.

I'm basically stranded here until he gets back. I'm too rattled to attempt to find the stairs. I don't want to do anything stupid that will land me back in the hospital, so I try to find some patience that I don't really possess. I count the seconds, since counting usually helps me calm myself. I'm at ninety-six when Mitchell returns.

"You okay?"

"We need to get something straight right now. You can

not keep asking me that just because I can't see. I'm already sick of it."

"Okay. I was actually referring to the effects of the vision you just had, though, not your blindness."

"Oh. Right." Maybe I'm a bit touchy right now. "I saw Isabelle asleep on the couch in front of the television."

"She liked to watch tapes of her old performances," Valentina says from somewhere behind Mitchell. "She knew exactly what every dismount sounded like. Every turn on the bars. It was like her sense of hearing and touch —everything other than sight—was...superhuman."

"That's how she was able to coach without seeing you girls, isn't it?" I ask.

"She's nodding," Mitchell tells me.

"Oh, sorry. I should be used to verbalizing everything after living with Isabelle, but to be honest, sometimes I wouldn't verbalize things on purpose."

"Your relationship with her was strained," I say.

"Not until after the accident. Before Isabelle lost her sight, we were close. She didn't only talk about gymnastics. But after... She wanted me to accomplish what she didn't get to, but I wasn't at the same level she was yet, so I had to catch up."

I can sense the truth coming off her in waves. "You didn't want to. Gymnastics wasn't your passion the way it was your sister's."

"No, it wasn't. But I felt so guilty that I could have what she wanted more than anything. I know that probably makes it seem like I'd quit gymnastics rather than live out Izzy's dream, but when I tried, she begged me to see this through. She said she'd be there with me every step of the way."

"You didn't want to take her dream from her all over again," I say.

Valentina starts to cry.

"Valentina, why did you have Isabelle's trophy in your room?" Mitchell asks. I'm assuming he's still holding the murder weapon.

"Isabelle told me to take it. She said I needed to look forward and visualize myself holding this trophy. It's from the competition right before the one..." She doesn't say the one Isabelle won before her accident, but I know that's what she means. "I kept refusing. I didn't want her trophies in my room, but after she died, I felt so guilty for arguing with her all the time. I thought taking the trophy and doing as she asked was the least I could do."

She had no idea she was removing the murder weapon from the crime scene. "Do you know which competition your sister was listening to Saturday night?"

"You mean the DVD?" Valentina's sobbing gets louder. "It was one of my competitions. She spent so much time studying my routines. Analyzing the way my footfalls hit the balance beam."

"Valentina, I told you to get your mother some water," Mr. DiMarco says.

"Is she okay?" Mitchell asks.

"She's awake and sitting on my daughter's bed. I'd like you both to leave. I understand you're doing your jobs, but we're mourning. Please keep your investigation to Isabelle's apartment. You need to allow us time to heal."

"Of course," Mitchell says. "I can't promise we won't have more questions for you, but we will do our best to conduct our investigation without you or your family present at the time."

"Thank you." Mr. DiMarco clears his throat.

Mitchell reaches for me, looping his arm around my waist, and helps me back down the stairs. The ambulance arrives before we leave, and Mitchell directs them upstairs before we head for his car.

"I need to bring this trophy to the station now that we know it's the murder weapon."

No one else at the station will question me when I tell them this is the murder weapon, but Detective O'Reilly won't believe it until the forensics team finds Isabelle DiMarco's blood on it. Still, they will find blood on it, so I'm fine with that.

Mitchell stops to get us something to eat on the way. We choose to eat in the car in the parking lot instead of inside the fast food place.

"I can't remember the last time I had a taco," I say.

"It's a good thing you can't see how much of it is ending up on your lap," Mitchell jokes. He uses a napkin to brush some food off my pants. "There. That's better."

"You're usually the messy eater," I say.

His energy feels off, like he's trying to force himself to make light conversation when something else is on his mind.

"You don't have to tiptoe around me, Mitchell. What is it you want to know?" I ask before finishing my third taco.

"I was just curious if you got a sense of the killer. By the way you raised the trophy in the air, I'm guessing you saw the vision from the killer's perspective."

"I did. It was weird, too."

"How so?" He slurps the rest of his ginger ale through his straw.

"Have you ever read 'The Tell-Tale Heart' by Edgar Allan Poe?"

"I did when I was in school, but I don't remember much other than the beating heart beneath the floorboards driving the killer to confess."

"That is what most people remember, but what always stuck with me is the calculated way the killer entered the old man's bedroom before he killed him. He was so careful not to make a sound."

"You're saying Isabelle's killer was the same way?"

"They had to be. According to Valentina, Isabelle's hearing was exceptional."

"That means the killer was well aware of Isabelle's strong sense of hearing." He slurps his drink again.

"I think that's finished, Mitchell."

"Sorry."

I hear the cup slide back into the holder in the middle console.

"Do you think it could be Valentina? I mean, she had the murder weapon," Mitchell says.

I'm not ruling out any possibilities yet. "The footfalls in my vision were really careful, and after what Valentina told us about how Isabelle would listen to the tapes to hear the footfalls on the balance beam, I think it's entirely possible the killer is a gymnast."

"I'm going to call your dad and see if he was able to get names for those two girls on the podium with Isabelle."

Dad would have called us if he had anything, but I know Mitchell wants to feel helpful and like we're making progress on the case, so I don't stop him.

"Hey, Mitchell," Dad says through the speaker. "I guess I wasn't working quickly enough for you."

"No, it's not that. Piper had a vision, and it points to the killer possibly being a gymnast. I think we're going to need more names than we thought. I'm talking about everyone at Isabelle's gym and gymnasts who competed with Isabelle before her accident. We'll need contact information for each as well."

"All right, but you get to explain to Bonnie why I'm missing our lunch date."

"He's teasing, Mitchell," Mom says. "I brought lunch to the office to eat with him so he can work."

"Hi, Mom. Hi, Dad," I say.

"Piper, I'm curious if you somehow did this to yourself

to get a break from seeing Mitchell after he's been suspended for two weeks," Dad teases.

I can't help smiling. "I won't lie. Getting to rest one of my senses isn't all that bad."

"Hey, are you saying you don't like looking at me?" Mitchell asks.

"She's only teasing you, Mitchell," Mom says. "Who wouldn't want to look at your handsome face?"

"Thank you, Mom," Mitchell says. "At least someone appreciates me."

"Getting back on track here," Dad says, "I do have something for you two. The girls on the podium are Skylar Harris and Phoebe Billings. They came in second and third to Isabelle in most competitions."

"Do they still live in town?" I ask.

"Actually, they do. Phoebe even coaches at the rival gym. It's called Rebel Gymnastics."

"Appropriate name," Mitchell says.

"Skylar stopped competing after she got injured and didn't make the Olympics."

"Injured like Isabelle?" I ask.

"Not quite. She broke her ankle. She was doing a complicated dismount from the uneven bars and landed funny. Well, it wasn't funny. That was a poor choice of words."

"We get it, Dad. I think we'll start with Phoebe since she's still part of the gymnastics world like Isabelle was."

"Sounds good. I'll get that list of names and contact information."

"Thanks, Dad. We'll be in touch," Mitchell says before ending the call.

"You ready to head to the station? I have to get the murder weapon to the forensics team."

I crumple up my wrapper. "Let's go."

When Mitchell walks me into the station, I can practically feel everyone's eyes on us. Harry must sense something is wrong with me because he comes right to my side.

"Hey, Harry." I bend down to pet him, and his nose immediately goes to my eyes. "You're a very smart boy."

"Piper, sorry about that. He never runs off," Officer Wallace says.

"It's okay. I think he sensed I could use a good seeing eye dog right about now."

"What?"

I sense others moving toward us. We have a captive audience.

"Piper had a vision, and the effect of it left her temporarily blind," Mitchell explains. "She did identify this as the object that Isabelle DiMarco was bludgeoned to death with."

"I can take that to forensics for you," Officer Gilbert says. He's still a rookie and very eager to please.

"Thanks, Gilbert."

I hear the tell-tale sounds of latex gloves being put on,

and then I smell Officer Gilbert's cologne as he takes the trophy from Mitchell.

"Piper, do you want to borrow Harry?" Officer Wallace asks. "He might be useful in your current condition."

I raise a hand until I find Mitchell's shoulder, which I pat. "I've got my own seeing eye dog right here, but I appreciate the offer Officer Wallace."

A few people chuckle at my joke.

"Thanks for that," Mitchell says.

"No problem." I smile in his general direction.

"You don't have any sight at all?" Detective O'Reilly asks.

"Detective, how are you doing?" I ask, avoiding her question.

"Today is my first day back. I'm on desk duty for a while since my recovery still has a way to go."

"You look like you're recovering quickly, though," Mitchell says. "You're getting around well."

"I was lucky."

"Yeah, you were. Considering you should have been wearing a bullet proof vest, you're lucky you're alive. Especially after you put Piper's life on the line." Mitchell is still upset with Detective O'Reilly for bringing me to confront a murderer without either of us wearing vests. I'm not sure he'll ever let that one go.

"I messed up. I can assure you it will never happen again," Detective O'Reilly says.

"Good."

I feel the air in front of my face move. "Are you testing my vision?" I ask.

"Sorry," she says. "I was just curious. You say this happened while working the case?"

"During a vision," Mitchell says, and I'm pretty sure it's just to annoy her since she doesn't think I actually have psychic visions. She thinks I have extremely good deductive reasoning skills that I try to pass off as psychic abilities.

Detective O'Reilly sighs.

"How do you explain her blindness?" Mitchell asks, putting her on the spot.

"There are plenty of possibilities for what caused this."

"Such as?" Mitchell challenges.

Detective O'Reilly shuffles her feet, and from the other faint sounds I'm hearing, I'm willing to bet she's crossed her arms. An almost inaudible groan accompanies the gesture. She's definitely still in some pain from the injury. "Piper suffers from frequent migraines. They can cause the blood vessels in the eyes to narrow and—"

"She doesn't have a migraine."

"Is she taking any medications? Some have side effects such as blindness," Detective O'Reilly says.

"Piper can't take medicine. She has adverse reactions to it." Mitchell's tone is making it very clear how frustrated he's getting. Unfortunately, Detective O'Reilly doesn't seem to notice.

"Adverse reactions like blindness?" she asks.

"No," I say. "I've already been examined at the hospital. There's nothing physically wrong with my eyes."

"It's an imagined condition?" Detective O'Reilly asks.

She's not completely wrong. "Sort of. Sometimes the effects of my visions are real, while other times they only seem real."

"Sounds like conversion disorder to me," she says. "The psychological stress of the case probably caused your temporary blindness."

"Brennan, Ashwell, my office," Chief Johansen bellows.

"Excuse us," I say as Mitchell leads me to the chief's office. He closes the door behind us. "Chief, good news. We've located the murder weapon. Forensics has it now."

"Good work. Hopefully, that's the clue we need because I'm pulling Piper from this case."

CHAPTER FIVE

This can't be happening. If I don't do something fast, Mitchell will get himself suspended again. "Chief," I say before Mitchell can speak, "I'm not leaving this case. If you remove me, I'll go to the family and get them to hire me. Mitchell might be my husband, but that won't stop me from solving this case before him and making the WPD look bad in the process for firing me."

The chief's chair rolls a few inches backward. "See why you don't need to fight her battles for her, Brennan?"

Mitchell laughs. "I do, sir. She's more than capable of handling herself."

"Even blind?" Chief Johansen asks. "Piper, I'm trying to protect you here. In your condition, it's not safe for you to pursue a killer. The last case almost got you killed. You're too valuable to this police department for me to sit back and allow something to happen to you."

"Chief, I have a feeling my lack of sight won't be an issue on this case."

"How can you say that? Mitchell is going to be so focused on you he might get either one of you shot."

"The killer didn't shoot Isabelle DiMarco. This was a crime of passion."

"I thought you said the killer was really calculated and careful. That points to this being premeditated."

"I don't think it was. I think this person went to Isabelle's, maybe to confront her about something, and they got really angry."

"You said Isabelle was asleep on the couch, so it wasn't Isabelle who made the killer angry."

"It could have been anything else in the apartment. The gymnastics DVD playing on the TV. The trophy itself." I shrug.

"I don't feel right keeping you on this case, Ashwell," Chief Johansen says. "I'm sorry, but I'm not going to change my mind."

"Chief, we've played this game before. It didn't end well for anyone involved. One of your detectives is still recovering from a gunshot. Let's not tempt history to repeat itself. I know what I'm doing. You need me on this case. I'm channeling Isabelle DiMarco to the point where I've taken on her loss of sight. You don't get any closer to a victim than that."

He's quiet for a moment. Then he says, "Can you have a vision of the future and tell me this all works out?"

Having visions of the future is where my abilities are the most limited. I do have them on rare occasions, but I can't make myself see the future. It has to happen on its own. "No, Chief. I can't. But I can tell you I'm supposed to solve this murder. I wouldn't have taken on the victim's blindness otherwise."

"You're putting me in a bad situation, Ashwell. I don't like it one bit."

"I understand that. I don't like not being able to see, but it is what it is. Neither of us asked for this, but we have to deal with it. Plain and simple."

The chief huffs. "I swear one of these days I'm going to transfer Brennan just to get the both of you out of my hair."

"That would be more threatening if you actually had hair." The chief has shaved his balding head for years.

Mitchell stiffens, his arm tightening around mine.

"Sorry, Chief. That sort of slipped out, but you do shave your head, so you can see my point."

"Both of you, out of my office now before you send me into early retirement."

Mitchell hurries me out.

"Well, I'm taking that comment to mean we're supposed to get back to work on this case."

Mitchell laughs. "I can't believe he let you get away with that."

"He feels guilty that this happened to me while I was

consulting on a case for him. I knew he wouldn't fire me. His energy was making that very clear."

"Well, next time maybe clue me in on that before you go saying something that might cost us both our jobs." He opens the car door for me.

"Where's the fun in that?" I ask, getting into the car and clicking my seat belt.

———

Mitchell drives us to Rebel Gymnastics, which is actually in the next town. It seems odd to check out Isabelle's rival gym before the one where she trained and worked, but it makes sense that the killer was someone who competed against Isabelle in some way.

Mitchell loops my arm through his and brings me inside. The noise level in the gym is intense. The soft thuds of landings on the mats. Hands clapping, most likely applying chalk for the uneven bars. Coaches shouting instructions. And then there's the energy in the room. Nervousness. Competitiveness. Drive. Desire to win. It's a lot to take in all at once. I'm usually better at keeping people's energy at bay until I come into physical contact with them, but my senses are working in overdrive to compensate for my lack of sight.

"Excuse me," Mitchell says to someone. "Can you tell us where we can find Phoebe Billings?"

"Who are you?" the girl asks.

"I'm Detective Brennan with the Weltunkin Police Department. This is my partner, Piper Ashwell."

"Police?" the girl asks. "Is this about Isabelle DiMarco?"

"Yes, did you know her?" Mitchell asks.

"Only by reputation."

Mitchell lets go of my arm, and I hear him grab his notepad and click his pen. "What's your name?"

"Am I in trouble? Am I a suspect?"

"Why do you think that?" Mitchell asks.

"I don't know. I've never talked to the police before. I don't know how this works."

"Just start with your name," I tell her.

"Um, Rhianna Foster."

"How old are you, Rhianna?" Mitchell asks.

"Seventeen."

"How long have you been with this gym?"

"Since I was five."

"And you've never met Isabelle at competitions?" Mitchell asks.

"Not officially, no. I've seen her there, but I never introduced myself or spoke to her."

"What's the rivalry like between Rebel Gymnastics and Extreme Gymnastics?" I ask.

"Oh, um...you know. We're each other's competition."

"So you're not close to anyone at Extreme?" I ask.

"I'm not. Tessa is, though. She's friends with Valentina DiMarco."

Interesting. That makes Tessa a link between the two gyms and possibly to Isabelle as well.

"Which one is Tessa?" Mitchell asks.

"Um, she's probably over by the balance beam right now." She pauses. I'm assuming to try to spot her teammate. "Yup. She's the one with the curly blonde ponytail and blue leotard."

"Thank you," Mitchell says before leading me that way. "Be careful. There's a lot to trip over in here with all the different sized mats."

"This is going to sound strange, but the sound bounces differently off the various objects, so I think I can actually tell what's around me without seeing it."

"You really are Bat Woman."

"Not loving that nickname, Mitchell."

"You're right. Piper Ashwell is superhuman all on her own." He gives my arm a gentile squeeze.

"Nice, Tessa. You were solid up until that landing. You really need to stick it if you want to place at the next meet."

"Excuse me," Mitchell says. "Are you Phoebe Billings?"

"No, I'm Julianna. Julianna Anderson." Her tone conveys her confusion.

"I'm Detective Brennan, and this is Piper Ashwell. We're looking for Phoebe."

"Phoebe didn't come in today."

Hmm, did she skip town after killing Isabelle? "When

did you last see her?" I ask, facing the general direction of Julianna's energy.

"Um, Saturday. She doesn't usually come to the gym on Sundays. It's her day off."

"But she's supposed to be here today?" Mitchell asks.

"Yeah, she called out sick. We take health very seriously around here. We can't have coaches passing on any germs to the gymnasts, so we don't come in if we think we might be coming down with something. It's better to be short on coaches than athletes."

"I see. Well, we're investigating the murder of Isabelle DiMarco. Did you know her?"

"Yes, I did." Her tone is somber. "It's just awful what happened to her. I mean her accident was bad enough. I can't believe..." She gets choked up. "I'm sorry. I didn't even know her all that well, but she was a legend. I followed her career. I could only dream of being the gymnast she was. It's so tragic what happened to her, and now..."

My senses are telling me Julianna's emotions are genuine. She respected and admired Isabelle. "We'd like to speak with Tessa for a moment if you don't mind," I say, hoping Mitchell will understand I believe Julianna is being truthful with us.

"Oh, um, she's a minor, you know. You might need her parents to be present."

We got away with that where Rhianna was concerned

since she openly talked to us. Mitchell can get in trouble for that, though.

"Is either of Tessa's parents here by chance?" Mitchell asks. "I see some parents in that room there with the glass."

"Yes, a lot of parents like to watch the practices. These girls are all elite athletes. Many, if not all, will even compete in the Olympics."

"Can you possibly get Tessa and her parents to meet us near the entrance? We certainly don't want to disturb anyone's training."

"I can do that," Julianna says.

Mitchell leads me back to the front of the gym. "I'm guessing you don't think she had anything to do with Isabelle's murder," he says once we're alone.

"No. She empathized with Isabelle."

"I got that impression, too. It's interesting that Tessa is friends with Isabelle's sister. I wouldn't think rival gyms would produce friends of any sort."

"It could be a source of tension for Tessa's or Valentina's teammates," I say. "But we were already planning to look into all the gymnasts from both places anyway."

"That's true. And that gives us another possible motive." Mitchell pauses. "Tessa and a man I'm assuming is her father are walking toward us now."

"We were told you wanted to speak to us," the man says.

Mitchell introduces us. "Can I get both of your full names, please?"

"I'm Liam Harris, and this is my daughter Tessa. Can I ask why you want to speak to us about Isabelle DiMarco?"

"We're questioning everyone at Extreme Gymnastics and Rebel Gymnastics," I say. "We want to talk to anyone who was close to Isabelle or worked with her."

"We understand Tessa is friends with Valentina DiMarco," Mitchell says.

"Yeah, we're good friends," Tessa says.

"Then I'm assuming you knew Isabelle better than the other girls at Rebel did," I say.

"I guess. I went to Tessa's house a lot, but Isabell had her own apartment in the detached garage."

"You didn't see her much then?" Mitchell asks.

"Not really, no. I saw her at competitions, though. She was usually with Valentina."

"Coaching her?" Mitchell asks.

"Yeah. She never really stopped coaching her."

"What do you mean by that?" Mitchell asks.

"Well, Valentina used to say she missed her sister. Isabelle started treating Valentina like any other gymnast. It hurt Valentina. She told me it was like she lost her sister when Isabelle lost her eyesight."

"That must have been difficult for her," I say.

"Tessa's been a good friend to Valentina," Mr. Harris says. "I've always admired how the two girls can be so close yet compete against each other. They're very professional in all the meets, yet they still congratulate each other when the competitions are over."

"That's very admirable," I say.

"Tessa, can you tell us more about Valentina's relationship with Isabelle?" Mitchell asks. I can't blame him for suspecting Valentina. She had the murder weapon in her room after all, and we know Isabelle was pushing Valentina to pursue a dream Valentina didn't want to strive for.

"It's okay, sweetheart," Mr. Harris says. "Just tell the truth."

"Valentina's my friend. I don't want to get her in any trouble."

"Why would you think you'd get her in trouble?" I ask.

"She and Isabelle fought a lot. Isabelle was really hard on Valentina. No matter how well Valentina did in a competition, Isabelle found something to criticize. I don't even think Valentina enjoyed gymnastics anymore. I wouldn't be surprised if she quit now that Isabelle is gone."

She won't.

Hmm. I shake my head, hoping Mitchell notices. I don't want to out myself as a psychic right now.

"Do you remember the last time you saw them fight?" Mitchell asks.

"Daddy," Tessa says.

"It's okay, sweetie," Mr. Harris says.

"Tessa, you're not doing anything wrong by telling us the truth," I say. "Withholding information from a police detective during an investigation is a problem, though. You don't want to get yourself in trouble for that. Please just tell us what you know, and I promise we will find out the full story. No matter what you say, it's not going to result in Valentina getting arrested."

"Do you think Valentina could have harmed her sister?" Mitchell asks her. "Is that why you're so worried?"

Tessa starts sobbing. "They fought Saturday morning. It was a huge fight. Valentina called me afterward. She told me..." She breaks down again.

I reach forward, sensing I might need to read her to figure out what Valentina said, but Tessa continues.

"She told me she wished Isabelle had died in that car accident."

CHAPTER SIX

Mitchell and I leave the gym after Tessa becomes inconsolable. It's clear Tessa's reached her limit, and her father isn't going to let us push her. We drive home because it's getting late. Mitchell orders dinner to be delivered to the apartment, and he walks Jez immediately.

I sit on the couch. Normally, I'd read to settle my mind after a long day of investigating, but I can't do that without the use of my eyes. I let out a deep breath and lean back on the couch cushion. I listen to all the sounds in the apartment. The hum of the refrigerator. The click of an ice cube falling into the tray, letting me know Mitchell turned the ice maker on. I can even hear the faint hum of electricity in the walls. I'm not sure I should be hearing that. It could be my psychic senses picking up on the energy. I'm literally experiencing the world the way Isabelle DiMarco did, which means I should be able to tune into her.

"Piper?" Mitchell's voice brings me to a more upright position.

"I was trying to sense Isabelle."

"Sorry for interrupting."

"It's okay. I'm not sure I would have been successful anyway."

"The food is here. I met the delivery guy downstairs as Jez and I were coming back into the building."

I turn my head toward him. "I didn't smell the food."

He sits down beside me, and the sound of plastic to-go containers sliding on the coffee table draws my attention.

"I can smell it now, but I should have smelled it as soon as you came into the apartment."

"You must really have been zoned out."

More like tuned in. Tuned in to Isabelle. "Did you turn on the ice maker?" I ask.

"No. We have a full tray of ice already."

"I heard an ice cube fall."

He places his hand on top of mine. "Piper, that's not possible. The refrigerator isn't making ice."

"Then that means Isabelle's was."

"But what does that mean? Is it important?"

"I don't know. I think I was hearing the sounds in her apartment."

"She was asleep, though. Do you think she heard them?"

"Unconsciously, yes."

"Wouldn't she have heard the killer then, too?"

"Maybe not. The killer was being so careful not to make a sound." I rub my head, trying to recall any other little details from my vision. "I don't remember hearing an ice maker in my vision, but if the sound was quiet enough, it's possible the killer didn't hear it, and that's why I didn't when I had the vision from the killer's perspective."

"Okay, that makes sense. It would also mean the ice tray must have been nearly full. Otherwise, the sound of the ice falling into the tray would have been much louder."

"I'm not sure why or even if any of this is important."

Mitchell lets go of my hand, and I hear the creak of a plastic lid being removed. "Here." He places the to-go container on my lap and then a fork in my hand. "You need to eat."

I take a bite of the pasta primavera.

"How is it?" Mitchell asks.

"Where's Jezebel?" I ask, ignoring his question about my food.

"In the kitchen eating her dinner."

"No, she's not. I'd hear her chewing. Mitchell, what's going on? Where's my dog?"

"She's in the bedroom."

I place my to-go container on the coffee table and stand up. "Why?" I start for the bedroom, knowing how to get around in the familiar space. I reach for the doorknob and open it. "Jez, come here."

She doesn't.

"Jezebel!"

Mitchell whistles, and I hear Jez jump down from the bed.

"She's sitting right in front of you," Mitchell says, coming to stand beside me.

"What did you do? Why was she avoiding me?"

"I didn't want her overwhelming you. As soon as we picked her up from your parents' house, she knew something was wrong with you. It made her very uneasy. That's why I brought her outside when we got home."

Jez is the model car passenger. She sits still and wears a seat belt. She probably had her eyes trained on me the entire time.

I bend down to scratch Jez behind the ears. "Mommy's okay, Jez."

She licks my left eye and then my right.

"I know. I can't see your beautiful face, but this won't last. I promise." I've never lied to my dog before, and truthfully, I hope I'm not lying. I hope this is only temporary.

———

Since Mitchell has to bring me everywhere, I can't get a moment's peace. It's worse than when he was suspended. I have to convince him I'm fine to shower, get dressed, and use the bathroom on my own. To say I'm in a bad mood Tuesday morning is a gross understatement.

"Coffee, lots of it," I tell Marcia as Mitchell and I step up to the counter.

"Marcia is giving you the once-over," Mitchell says.

The way he narrates life for me is also getting on my nerves. It's like I'm walking around in a crime movie complete with a voice-over narrator.

"Piper, why can't you see?" Marcia asks.

I wave a hand in the air. "Stupid side effect of a vision. Our victim was blind."

Her footsteps stomp around the counter, and she pulls me in for a hug. "Don't even try telling me you don't like to be hugged."

I hug her back instead. "I appreciate your concern, but I'm fine. This one doesn't let me do anything on my own, though, so you may need to come visit me in jail after I murder him."

Marcia pulls away from me, holding me at arm's length. "Please, you could totally get away with murder between your investigative know-how and your psychic abilities. You'd be fine."

"Hey, she's talking about murdering *me*," Mitchell says. "Did you miss that part?"

"Come on, Mitchell. You should know better than to baby her. Piper, I'll get you two coffees. Mitchell, you better hope I don't put sleeping pills in your coffee so Piper can get a break from you."

"What did I do? I'm only trying to help my wife."

"Try backing off unless she asks for your help," Marcia says. "Now, Piper, what do you feel like eating this morning?"

"Hmm, I don't know why, but I really want a jelly donut."

"Jelly donuts coming right up."

The bell above the door jingles as someone walks into Marcia's Nook.

"I asked Valentina to meet us here. That's her now," Mitchell whispers to me.

"When did you do that?"

"While you were getting dressed."

I'm surprised she agreed to talk to us without her parents present.

"Hi. I only have half an hour before I have to get to the gym," Valentina says.

"Please sit. What can I get for you?" Mitchell asks her.

A chair slides across the floor as she sits. "Oh, I can't eat anything. I'm on a strict diet."

"Here you go. I gave you six jelly donuts. On the house. I'll bring the coffees to your table," Marcia says.

I grab the box of donuts from the counter, and Mitchell takes my arm to lead me to the nearest table. I open the box and immediately bite into a donut.

"Those were Isabelle's favorite. She used to sneak them every once in a while." I can hear the smile in Valentina's voice.

"You mean when she was still competing," I say.

"Yeah." Her tone changes, and I can feel her loss.

I can't help wondering if my sudden craving for jelly

donuts has anything to do with me channeling Isabelle DiMarco. It would make sense.

"Valentina, I have sort of a strange question I'd like to ask you."

"Okay?" It comes out more like a question.

"Do you know if your sister's ice maker was on Saturday night?"

"Probably. Isabelle was big on icing injuries. She busted up her knee pretty badly in that car accident. It still bothered her years later. She usually iced it at night. Her ice maker was typically running to refill the tray."

So it's possible I really was hearing sounds from Isabelle's apartment last night.

"Why do you ask?" Valentina says.

"Here you go," Marcia says. "Can I get something for you?"

"No, thank you. I'm good," Valentina says.

"All right. Let me know if you need anything else," Marcia says before walking away.

"Piper and I are trying to retrace your sister's step Saturday evening," Mitchell says, picking back up with the conversation.

"Well, I can tell you what she usually did in the evenings."

"That would be helpful," Mitchell says. He clicks his pen.

"Isabelle iced her knee every night and listened to DVDs of practices and competitions. She used to listen to her own, but about three years ago, she switched to solely analyzing mine."

"You don't sound too happy about that," I say before taking another bite of the jelly donut.

"That's when things started getting bad between us. She stopped viewing me as her sister. I was just someone she coached."

"Tessa Harris said you called her Saturday morning because you were upset about a fight you'd had with Isabelle."

"Tessa said that?" Valentina sounds completely surprised.

"Is it not true?" Mitchell asks.

"No, it is, but I'm surprised she told you."

"Why?" I ask.

"Tessa's not a gossip. That's why I like her. The other girls at Rebel like to talk trash. But Tessa is different."

"She wasn't trying to get you in trouble," I say. "She didn't want to talk to us about you at all. She seems protective of you."

"You see, Valentina, withholding information from the police can get you in a lot of trouble. Tessa told us about the fight because she didn't want to get in trouble for interfering with an open investigation."

"She told us how tough Isabelle was on you, and how much you missed the relationship you once had with your sister."

"What did you two fight about on Saturday?" Mitchell asks.

"The usual. She never thinks I'm putting in enough time or effort. She lived at the gym when she was competing, but I have a life outside of gymnastics. I don't want this to be my whole life. I'm not like Izzy." She scoffs. "I tried to tell her I wanted to be well-rounded. She told me that was a nice way of saying unfocused. Then she accused me of not being grateful for the opportunities I have that others don't. By others, she meant herself. She always had to make me feel guilty for her accident. I kept trying to tell her that it wasn't my fault that truck hit her. An accident is just that. An accident. No one is to blame."

Not true.

"She's lying?" I ask my senses.

"Who? Izzy?" Valentina asks.

"No, I think Piper is sensing that you're lying to us right now."

"I'm not sure. My senses just said 'Not true,' but I don't know exactly what's not true."

"Your senses talk?" Valentina asks, and she couldn't sound more confused.

"Sort of. It's hard to explain."

A chair scrapes against the floor. "Look, I really need to go if I'm going to make it to the gym on time."

"We'll probably see you there later," Mitchell says. "We want to check out the place and the people Isabelle worked with and trained."

"Great." Her tone doesn't match her word choice at all. Her footsteps are light and quick across the floor.

"What did you make of that?"

I sip my coffee. "I don't know. I wish my senses would have been clearer."

"Want to go to your office and hash all this out with your dad?"

"Yeah, we should order a coffee for him."

"Marcia, already brought it."

I stand up.

"I'll take our things." There's a familiar squeak of coffee cups sliding into the drink caddy. Then it gets quiet. I'm sure Mitchell is debating whether or not to help me out of Marcia's Nook. This place is like my second home, though. I walk around the table and toward the door. Mitchell opens the door for me.

"After you," he says.

I count the twenty-three steps back to my office. Who knew one day my incessant counting would help me get around when I couldn't see where I was going?

"Oh, there you two are," Dad says. "I was just about to go to Marcia's Nook to find you. Go on in, pumpkin. I've got the door."

I step into the office. I don't know if Mitchell pushed in the chair in front of my desk, and I don't want to trip over it, so I reach out with my hand. I hear the chair slide across the floor out of my way. "Thank you, Mitchell," I say, knowing he was the one who moved it.

"Sorry."

"No, it's fine. I know you're only trying to help. I just hate feeling helpless." I place my left hand on my desk to feel my way around it to my chair.

"You're far from helpless."

"Jelly donuts?" Dad asks.

"Yeah, Piper had a craving, and as it turns out, our victim happened to love jelly donuts," Mitchell says.

"You're channeling her, pumpkin."

"The loss of vision thing sort of already implied that."

"Drink your coffee," Dad says. "Caffeine-deprived Piper is never fun to deal with."

"Sorry." I reach for my coffee, which miraculously winds up in my hand. "Thanks, Mitchell."

"What?" he feigns innocence.

"We need to find Phoebe Billings. She called out of the gym sick yesterday. We need to find out if she's really sick or if she ran because she's the killer."

"I have some home addresses for those people you had me look up," Dad says. A paper slides across the desk.

"Great. I'm not convinced Valentina isn't the guilty party, but we definitely need to see who else had motive."

"You really think a seventeen-year-old girl brutally murdered her sister?" Dad sounds horrified by the idea.

"She was harboring a lot of animosity toward Isabelle. I think it's possible she did this."

Valentina is familiar with both Isabelle's routine and

her apartment. It gives her means, motive, and opportunity. I can see why Mitchell is leaning in that direction.

"Pumpkin, did you sense anything about the killer?" Dad asks.

"They're extremely patient, meticulous, careful, and they had plenty of rage."

"Valentina," Mitchell says.

Everything seems to point to her, but when are our cases ever that easy to solve? Something isn't right here.

CHAPTER SEVEN

"Piper, you're making a face," Dad says.

I finish my first coffee and start on my second, needing the jolt of caffeine to fuel my brain. "I don't know what it is, but something isn't sitting right with me."

"All the pieces lining up is causing you to feel uncomfortable?" Mitchel asks.

"We've barely talked to any suspects. This case can't be that simple."

"We found the murder weapon in her room."

"I believed Valentina's explanation for that. I didn't sense she was being dishonest."

My visions always point me to clues whether I realize it right away or not. "None of my visions showed Valentina. If she's the killer, I think I would have seen her."

"What is it, Mitchell?" Dad asks.

I can't see Mitchell's expression, but he must have thought of something.

"This is going to sound crazy, but what if Piper lost her eyesight because Isabelle doesn't want her murder to be solved?"

"That's absurd. Isabelle's spirit didn't blind me, Mitchell. This is me channeling her because of my vision. My senses did this, and they wouldn't stop me from seeing who the killer is. They don't work that way."

"Okay." To his credit, he doesn't ever need proof where I'm concerned. He's always believed me without a single shred of evidence. "What do we do next then?"

"If I were you, I'd look into the two girls Piper saw on the podium: Skylar Harris and Phoebe Billings," Dad says.

"Mitchell, we're idiots," I say, not sure how I didn't realize this sooner.

"What are you talking about?" he asks.

"Skylar Harris. Tessa Harris."

"Oh. You think they're related."

"It's not an uncommon last name," Dad says, but let's find out. "They could be sisters or cousins." His fingers click across the keyboard. "Look at that. Tessa is Skylar's younger sister."

Hmm. "The families seem to be friendly. I mean Tessa and Valentina are good friends. I wonder if Skylar and Isabelle were, too, but they put up a front during competitions to throw people off."

"Is that what you're sensing?" Mitchell asks.

"No, I'm hypothesizing."

"It is a good theory," Dad says.

"It's also possible that Skylar eventually got upset losing to Isabelle all the time. Maybe that's what I was sensing when I read that trophy."

"Another good theory," Dad says. "Why don't you start with her?"

"Dad, can you check out the social media posts for all of the gymnasts' names we gave you? See if any of them mention Isabelle."

"I'm on it. Let me warn you two not to be late for dinner tonight. Your mother is making a turkey."

"It's not even close to Thanksgiving," I say.

"I know, but she found this new recipe, and she wants to try it out. You know how I feel about dry turkey, so don't be late no matter what."

"He's wagging his finger at us, isn't he?" I ask Mitchell.

"Yup."

I stand up and meet Mitchell on the other side of my desk. "We'll see you at dinner, Dad. Feel free to cut out after you finish your social media search."

"Do you have any idea how long it's going to take me to look through teenage girls' posts? I think I have a headache already."

"Well, at least they're committed gymnasts. The selfies should be minimal. I'm betting it will be more pictures of competitions and such," Mitchell says.

"I hope so. If you've seen one teenage girl making a

duck face, you've seen them all. Why do they think that looks good, anyway? Am I just too old to get it?"

I laugh. "Have fun, Dad." I reach for Mitchell, who already has his arm out for me.

"Your car is still parked here. We should really get it home soon."

"No one will touch it here. It's fine."

He helps me into the patrol car. "Skylar lives in a really nice gated community. I'm ashamed to admit I'm glad you won't see how nice her house probably is. I doubt I'll ever be able to afford anything like that for us."

"I happen to hate big homes. Too much to clean, so even if I could see, you'd be perfectly safe."

"Good to know."

Mitchell's reaction when we pull up to the gate tells me all I need to know. Certain areas of Weltunkin are extremely wealthy. This is definitely one of them. He introduces himself to the guard, and I'm sure he flashes his badge because he loves any excuse to whip that out from under his shirt where he wears it on a chain.

"And we're in," Mitchell says as he pulls through the gate.

"Phew. I'm so glad you told me because the moving vehicle did not make that clear."

"Sorry. I don't mean to give you a play-by-play on everything. I just know I'd be going crazy if I couldn't see everything around me. Mostly you, though. Not being able to see your face would be the ultimate torture."

I reach for his leg and give it a gentle squeeze. He has his moments when he's really sweet.

"I think this is it," Mitchell says. He pulls up a driveway and parks.

"They live on a hill," I say.

"Yeah, and the view is absolutely breathtaking." He places his hand on mine. "Sorry, that was insensitive."

"No, it's fine. I prefer when you act normally and don't try to censor yourself where my eyesight is concerned."

He opens his door. "I notice you said where your eyesight is concerned."

I laugh. "You picked up on that, huh?" I reach for my door, locating the handle and opening it. Mitchell is at my side as I step out of the car, which I actually do appreciate since I've never been to Skylar Harris's home before.

Mitchell leads me to the front door. "Are you curious what this place looks like?"

"Let me guess. It's beautifully landscaped with those trees that look like spirals and other shapes. There are flowers and other colorful trees. The driveway is probably circular near the top. We're on a hill, so I'm going to say no horses." I hold up a finger. "Unless their property extends down the hill where the horses are kept." We encountered a property like that on the first case we worked together.

"I don't see any stables," Mitchell says. "Keep going, though. You're doing surprisingly well."

"The house is probably white. I'm going to guess

there's a balcony on at least one bedroom on the second floor. Three-car garage. Inground pool around back. Huge back patio for entertaining. Probably some sort of fireplace out there as well."

"I can't see the back of the house, but I'm going to assume you're right about most of that since you were spot-on with the front of the house." We stop walking. "Are you sure you can't see? This isn't just a ruse to get me to do things for you, is it?"

"Yes, that's so typical for me. Wanting other people to invade my space and do things for me."

"All right, point well taken," he says before ringing the doorbell.

The door creaks open, but no one says anything for a moment.

"Are you Mrs. Harris?" Mitchell finally asks.

"Yes." I reach out with my senses, trying to gauge her emotional state at the moment.

"I'm Detective Brennan with the Weltunkin PD. This is my partner, Piper Ashwell. We'd like to ask you a few questions and possibly speak to Skylar if she's home."

"Skylar drove Tessa to the gym. She should be back soon, but I'm not sure I like the idea of the police questioning my daughter."

"While I understand your concern, Skylar is a legal adult," Mitchell says. "She's twenty-three, isn't she?"

"She is, but that's still a baby in my eyes." I can feel the woman's stare, and I realize what has her confused.

"I'm temporarily blind," I say. "I'm sorry if I'm not looking directly at you. I don't mean to make you uncomfortable."

"Temporarily blind?" she asks.

"Yes, I should be fine soon."

"Oh, well, that's good." She sighs. "Can I ask what this is about before I invite you into my home? I don't remember receiving a call from the police station."

"You didn't. We're investigating the murder of Isabell DiMarco, and we're talking to everyone who had contact with her."

"I thought you said you wanted to speak with Skylar. Skylar hasn't talked to Isabelle in years. And there's no way I'm allowing you to question Tessa. She's a minor."

"We've already spoken to Tessa and your husband at Rebel Gymnastics," Mitchell says, his tone full of confusion.

"Your husband didn't tell you that. He didn't tell you anything about it," I say.

"No, he did not." Annoyance fills her voice.

"Well, we're just trying to talk to everyone from both Rebel and Extreme."

"Then why do you want to talk to Skylar? Like I said, Skylar and Isabelle haven't talked in years. They were competitors at one time, but they haven't been in contact since Isabelle's car accident."

"Really?" I ask. "How is that possible when Isabelle

was coaching? And Tessa and Valentina are friends. How would Isabelle and Skylar never cross paths?"

"I suppose they might have at competitions, but I assure you they never stopped to talk to one another."

"Why are you so sure of that?" Mitchell asks. "Was there bad blood between Isabelle and Skylar?"

"What exactly are you implying?" Mrs. Harris asks.

"I think what Detective Brennan means is that there must be some reason for two young women who grew up in the gymnastics world together and have sisters who are friends to not speak to each other."

"Mrs. Harris, I'll be honest with you. You seem very resistant to our questions, and that's not painting your daughter in a very good light right now."

The sound of a car engine behind us makes me turn, out of habit since I can't see who it is.

"Is that Skylar now?" Mitchell asks.

"Yes."

The beep of a car lock is followed by heels on the driveway. Skylar must be dressed up. Why would she wear heels to take her sister to the gym?

"Mom, what's going on?" Skylar asks.

"These detectives are asking questions about Isabelle," Mrs. Harris says.

"Oh. Yeah, I heard what happened to her. It's awful."

Mitchell steps back, pulling me with him, and then I smell Skylar's perfume as she walks past us. I have to stifle a sneeze.

"Come in," Skylar says.

"Skylar, I don't think we should be inviting them in. I still don't understand why they're here."

"They're doing their jobs, Mom. Someone killed Isabelle. They need to find the guilty party. Tessa said Valentina and her parents aren't doing well. They need closure." The next thing she says is directed to Mitchell and me. "Please come in and make yourselves comfortable."

"Thank you," Mitchell says. He leads me inside. "Your home is beautiful."

"Mom, why don't you go make some tea?" Skylar says.

Their dynamic is interesting. Skylar is acting more like the mother, and Mrs. Harris is playing the part of the obedient daughter. I also get the sense this is their typical way of interacting.

Footsteps sound across the floor, getting fainter as they move away from us.

"Sorry about her. She's really overprotective." Skylar starts walking, and we follow, Mitchell leading me by my arm. He pulls me down onto a couch.

"Thank you for agreeing to speak with us like this," Mitchell says. "We're trying to question everyone informally at the moment."

"I understand. Tessa told me she spoke to you."

Interesting that Skylar knew but her mother didn't. Is there something about Mrs. Harris that makes her incapable of handling certain things? I would love to read her to find out.

"Skylar, it seems like your sister and father purposely kept the investigation from your mother," I say.

"Yeah. That's because they did. Mom can't handle stuff like this."

"Why is that?" I ask.

"First, can I ask you a question?" Skylar seems to be speaking directly to me now.

"My eyesight is temporarily nonexistent," I say.

"I thought so. I mean the way you look and act, it reminds me of Isabelle after her accident."

"According to your mother, you and Isabelle haven't spoken to one another since that accident," Mitchell says.

"That's not exactly true. The accident was really tough on Mom. She was driving behind Isabelle when it happened. She saw the whole thing. It really shook her up, and she hasn't been the same since. We weren't allowed to even mention Isabelle's name, so I stopped talking to her."

"Wait. Are you saying you and Isabelle were friends at one time?" Mitchell asks.

"Not friends, no. We were friendly to each other, though. I mean we were competitors, and I wanted to beat her, but I didn't hate her or anything. We would talk."

I don't want to tell her I saw her and Skylar with Isabelle in a vision, so I opt for a different approach. "Isabelle had tapes of all her competitions. I couldn't help noticing you were not happy coming in second place to her."

"I guess your loss of eyesight was recent," she says.

I nod.

She sighs. "You're not wrong. I was upset about always losing to Isabelle, but then I realized she was at the gym twenty-four seven. I didn't want that life."

She sounds like Valentina.

"I finally came to terms with the fact that losing to Isabelle wasn't Isabelle's fault. It was mine. I wasn't willing to give every second of every day to gymnastics. In the end, it just didn't matter as much to me as it did to her."

"That's very mature of you," Mitchell says.

"I don't know. I was a kid at the time. It took me a while to come to that realization, but I believe Isabelle got what she deserved."

Truth.

"When did you last see Isabelle?" Mitchell asks.

"Um, in passing when I dropped off Tessa at Valentina's house. I think that was Friday night."

"Did you speak to her?" Mitchell asks.

"No. She was going into her apartment. I admit I watched her. It was impressive how well she got around. She used one of those walking canes you see blind people with. I swear she was good at everything."

I sense jealousy, but it quickly fades. Maybe it's left over from the days when they competed.

"Do you know if Isabelle had any enemies?" Mitchell asks.

"No. Most people liked her. She was pretty tough on the girls she trained, though. Valentina cried to Tessa a lot."

Everything seems to lead back there. "What about Phoebe Billings?" I ask.

"Phoebe competed long after I stopped. I haven't seen or talked to her in years, so I don't know if she and Isabelle were in contact. I doubt it, though. Phoebe hated Isabelle. She hated me, too."

"How did that work?" Mitchell asks. "I mean she's your sister's coach, isn't she?"

"Yeah. That's why I drop Tess off outside. I don't go inside the gym. Phoebe can be...intense."

"Do you think Phoebe would ever harm Isabelle?" Mitchell asks.

Skylar lets out a deep breath. "I don't know, and I don't want to speculate about something like that." Her phone rings. "Sorry, I have to take this. It's my dad. He's on a hunting trip."

"We'll see ourselves out. Thank you again for your time," Mitchell says.

I stand up and follow him to the door. "Looks like we need to find Phoebe Billings," I whisper to him.

"My thoughts exactly."

CHAPTER EIGHT

Mitchell calls Rebel Gymnastics on the way to the gym.

"Rebel Gymnastics, this is Rochelle speaking. How can I help you?" comes a sickeningly sweet voice through the Bluetooth.

"Hello, I'm calling to find out if Phoebe Billings is at the gym today."

"One moment please." There's silence on the other end of the line.

"If she's still a no-show, she's going to look extremely guilty in my eyes," Mitchell says.

I can't argue with him there. Unless she really is sick. It could be a coincidence that she got sick right after Isabelle was murdered.

"Sir?" the woman says.

"Yes, I'm here."

"Ms. Billings is busy coaching at the moment. She asked me to take a message."

I turn to smile at Mitchell.

"No message," he says. "Thank you anyway."

He accelerates, in a hurry to get to the gym. He never told the woman who answered the phone that he's a police detective, but since we've already been to the gym and questioned several people in regard to Isabelle DiMarco's murder, it wouldn't take much for Phoebe Billings to figure out that's who called looking for her. She might try to make a run for it before we arrive.

"When we get there, you should go find Phoebe. Don't give her the chance to run. I'll only slow you down."

"Piper, I'm not going anywhere without you. You're my partner. You wouldn't leave me behind if the situation was reversed."

We make it to the gym, and Mitchell parks the car. "I got a spot up front. Let's go."

We both scramble out of the car, and he meets me around the front, where he takes my arm.

All the sounds and emotions of last time hit me again the second we walk inside.

"I see a coach with red hair," Mitchell tells me.

"Great. Direct me to her."

"She's by the balance beam."

Balance beam.

"Hmm."

"What?" he asks.

"My senses just said balance beam."

"You think it's important?"

"It must be, but I don't know why." Isabelle didn't die at the gym, and she never even trained here.

"Are you going to try to read it?"

"I guess I have to."

"Step up. There's a mat about two feet tall."

"Whoa! Hold up!" an authoritative voice yells. "You can't wear street shoes on there!"

Mitchell and I stop. "Are you Phoebe Billings?" he asks her.

"Yeah."

"I'm Detective Brennan, and this is Piper Ashwell. We need to ask you a few questions in private."

"I'm a little busy here at the moment."

"Well, you can talk to us here right now, or I can haul you down to the police station. Your call." He's not messing around or allowing her time to run.

"Coach Anderson!" the young woman bellows. "I need you to cover beam. Ruby's having trouble sticking her dismount."

"I'm on it," Julianna Anderson says. I can already tell I'm not going to like Phoebe as much as I liked Julianna. They seem to have completely different personalities.

"This way," Phoebe says, and Mitchell helps me follow her. My foot gets caught on the edge of a mat, but Mitchell grabs me before I fall.

"What's wrong with her?" Phoebe asks, no sympathy at all in her tone.

"Just blind. Don't mind me," I say, filling my voice with sarcasm.

"Seriously? How does that work? You can't exactly investigate when you can't see anything."

I could grab her hand and see all I want to. I'm tempted to do exactly that, but Phoebe strikes me as the type to take a swing at my head if I touch her without asking. Actually, she might take a swing at me even if I do ask. "I manage," is all I say.

I hear a door close behind us.

"Last time we were here, the gymnasts' parents were in this room," Mitchell says.

"It's a closed practice today. No spectators."

"I see. Getting ready for a big competition."

"Exactly, so can we hurry this along?"

"If you're so worried about the upcoming competition, why weren't you here yesterday?" I ask her.

"I was sick."

"You don't look like you're sick," Mitchell says. "What exactly was wrong with you?"

"I had a stomach thing. It was probably something I ate, but you don't take chances with athletes like this. I couldn't risk passing on any germs and keeping someone from competing."

"How would you describe your relationship with Isabelle DiMarco?" Mitchell asks.

"We didn't have one. Isabelle was my competition growing up. She got injured in a car accident and stopped competing. End of story."

"Not really," I say. "You both wound up coaching at rival gyms. I'm sure you ran into each other."

"Not that she'd know. She was blind."

This girl is really getting on my nerves. "You think because she couldn't literally see your face, she didn't know you were at the competitions with her? You can't possibly be that stupid."

"Easy," Mitchell whispers, placing his hand on mine. "I think what Piper means is that people who have no sense of sight tend to compensate for it with their other senses."

Phoebe laughs. "Right. So she smelled me like a dog?"

I've had it with her. I take a step in her direction, but Mitchell holds me back.

"What are you going to do? You can't even see me."

I hold out my right hand, not touching her, but trying to read her without making physical contact. I can sense her anger, but that's about all.

"What are you doing?" Phoebe asks me.

"Piper happens to be psychic," Mitchell says. "She's finding out all we need to know about you right now."

He's overselling my abilities, but I appreciate it because it makes Phoebe so angry she swats at my hand. The subtle shift in the air alerts me to her movement in time for me to grab her hand.

"I'm not going to lose to Isabelle DiMarco again. Stick your landing, Ruby, or so help me I will find someone else who can!"

Mitchell yanks us apart and stands between us. "If you take another swing at my partner, I will haul you out of here in handcuffs. Am I making myself clear?"

"She grabbed me," Phoebe says.

"She stopped you from hitting her. That's self-defense," Mitchell says, covering for what I was actually doing.

"It must have been hard losing to Isabelle when you two competed head to head. And then she was a better coach than you, even without her eyesight. That drove you crazy, didn't it? That's why you were making all those comments about being blind. You're bitter that her loss of sight didn't stop her from beating you like she always did."

"I'm done talking to you."

"Would you like to lawyer up?" I ask. "Go right ahead, but it will only make you look even guiltier. Right now, you're our top suspect."

Phoebe scoffs. "You've got to be kidding me. Sure, I hated Isabelle, but I had no reason to kill her. She wasn't a threat to me or anyone else. She was basically a waste of space."

"If she wasn't a threat to you, why did you tell Ruby you weren't going to lose to Isabelle again, and you'd replace Ruby if you had to?"

"You can't possibly know..." She stops, and I wish I could see what she was doing.

"I read you," I say. "You really shouldn't have taken that swing at me. I see just fine in my visions."

"She can't do that against my will. That has to be illegal," Phoebe tells Mitchell.

"Like I said. You tried to hit Piper. Piper is entitled to defend herself. The only person to blame for her reading you is you. She can't always control when her visions hit. Physical contact is what brings them on."

"This isn't fair."

"Fair or not, you'd better start explaining yourself. I'd start with where you were Saturday night, and who can verify your story."

"I was on a date."

"Until what time?" Mitchell asks.

"I don't know. Eleven thirty. Sometime around then."

"Which would allow you to get to Isabelle's place and murder her a little after midnight," I say.

"I didn't kill her."

"Can anyone verify your whereabouts at midnight?" Mitchell asks.

"No. I was home alone."

"Too bad. Looks like you don't have an alibi then," I say.

"This is absurd. You have no proof of anything. You can't link me to this murder. You need evidence if you're going to charge me with something, and you have none."

"We'll get it," Mitchell says. "You can count on it." He takes my arm and loops it through his. "Piper, I think we're finished here for now, but I wouldn't plan to leave town anytime soon, Phoebe. We'll be back."

"I bet Isabelle could've helped Ruby stick that dismount," I say on our way out.

"Ugh!" Phoebe yells behind us.

"She's got quite the temper," I say.

"Yeah, and you have a talent for pushing people's buttons."

"It's a gift."

"You know when we first started working together, I thought it was your lack of people skills that made you rile up suspects like that, but now I'm starting to think you've known what you were doing all along."

It was definitely my lack of people skills. I've gotten better since working with Mitchell, so maybe now I do it more for the reactions.

"Where's the balance beam?" I ask Mitchell.

"You still want to read it?"

"I do, but what are the odds they're going to let us near it? It's a closed gym, and Phoebe is currently coaching Ruby on it."

"Well, actually Julianna Anderson is coaching Ruby on it at the moment."

Something still seems wrong to me. Isabelle never used this beam. Why are my senses telling me to read it?

"Maybe I could pretend to slip on the edge of the mat and read it when I accidentally fall onto it."

"If you could see and make sure that happened that way, I'd say it was a good plan, but I'm not sure it's doable in your current condition."

"We have to try, Mitchell. You can direct me."

He squeezes my arm tighter to his side, the opposite of what I need him to do. "How do you explain me letting go of you?"

"Pretend to tie your shoe or something."

He shuffles his feet.

"What are you doing?"

"Trying to loosen my laces with my other foot."

"Are we heading toward the beam?"

"Yes. It's about twenty feet in front of us. The mat surrounds it, though, which means you'll need to stumble about six feet before you reach any part of the balance beam."

"Got it."

"Are you sure about this?"

"Mitchell, I've been counting feet all my life to center myself. I was born to do this."

"Okay good, because we're five feet away." He loosens his grip on me, and I hear the faint rustle of his clothing as he bends down.

I reach out with my senses for the objects around me. My foot hits the mat, and I stumble, careful to step up onto the mat. I reach out with my hands, searching for the beam to grab onto. Like Mitchell said, it's about six feet away. I find it and latch on.

"Tessa, you have to get Valentina to tell you about her routine. We need to know what we're up against," Phoebe says.

Tessa is straddling the beam. "That's cheating."

"No. Spying on her would be cheating. Getting her to tell you is a completely different story."

"Isabelle would kill Valentina if she told me. And my sister would lose all respect for me if I won that way."

"Piper, are you okay?" Mitchell asks at my side.

Everyone must be gathered around me if he pulled me from the vision.

"You need to leave," Phoebe says.

"Coach Anderson, you should know Phoebe was trying to convince Tessa to find out what Valentina's routine on beam is. Tessa refused. If I were you, I'd get rid of Phoebe before she ruins this gym's reputation altogether."

Phoebe yells, and the next thing I know, Mitchell lets go of me, and there's a scramble on the mat.

"Phoebe Billings, you're under arrest for attempted assault," Mitchell says.

CHAPTER NINE

With Phoebe now in police custody, it allows us time to find evidence to prove she killed Isabelle. The rage I felt from her certainly matches the rage I felt from the killer. But she was right when she said we had no evidence to pin this on her. We don't.

"Forensics found traces of Isabelle's blood on the trophy, but the only prints on it belong to you, me, and Valentina DiMarco," Mitchell says as we sit at his desk at the police station.

"You have to question Valentina again," I say, knowing procedure calls for it.

"I do, but there's still the possibility that the killer wiped their prints off the trophy."

"That means whatever the killer used to wipe the trophy is still out there somewhere."

"Unless they burned it," Detective O'Reilly says, coming up behind me.

I don't bother to turn in her direction since I can't see her anyway.

"Someone making a fire this time of year might be a little suspicious," Mitchell says.

"Not if they have one of those fire pits. A lot of people do," she says. "But, if the sister's prints are on the murder weapon..." Detective O'Reilly likes things to be black and white. No gray area at all. Of course, she'd blame Valentina DiMarco.

"Thanks for your input, Detective," Mitchell says, and it's clear it's a dismissal.

Detective O'Reilly clears her throat. "Right. Well, good luck."

"She wants your approval," I say.

"She has a lot to make up for in my mind." Mitchell isn't going to forgive her anytime soon.

"What time is it?" I ask.

"Time for dinner." Mitchell's voice is panicked. "We need to go right now, or we'll be late."

We rush out of there. Since we have one suspect in custody, and the other is a minor who needs a lawyer present, we're at a standstill. Mitchell calls the DiMarco family on the way to let them know Valentina will be questioned tomorrow morning at ten. Mitchell handles it well, explaining Valentina's prints on the murder weapon make this conversation necessary and that she should have representation with her. Looks like our morning is planned for us.

Mom greets us at the door. "With three seconds to spare. Cutting it close, you two."

"It was a busy day," I say, stepping into the house. Since I grew up here, I know my way around in the dark, which means moving around blindly shouldn't be an issue for me. I head right for the dining room since I can smell the turkey.

"This looks incredible. It's just like Thanksgiving," Mitchell says, pulling out my chair for me.

"It smells great, Mom," I say.

She gives me a hug. "I won't ask how you're doing," she says. "I know my girl is tough."

I can't exactly fix myself a plate, so I let Mitchell do it for me. Jezebel places her head in my lap. She's still acting so somber around me, which is odd. I'm used to her being so happy and excited to see me. I pet her head. "No turkey for dogs. Sorry, Jez and Max."

Max is my parents' dog. He was a little terror before Jez came along and whipped him into shape. I think Mom likes watching Jez every day because Jez essentially watches Max and keeps him out of trouble. He's become a really good dog because of Jez.

Jezebel licks my arm and puts her head back in my lap.

"I feel bad. I think my blindness is the first thing Jez doesn't fully comprehend." I've never met a dog who understands human speech to the extent that Jezebel does. But she's sufficiently stumped right now.

"She'll be okay, pumpkin," Dad says. "Any sign of your vision returning?"

"No. I can see lights, but that's about it."

"If reading something of Isabelle's caused this, maybe reading something else of hers will undo it," Mom says.

Mitchell places my plate down in front of me. "Dig in."

I pick up my fork. I fumble a little, but I manage to cut my turkey and eat it. "After we talk to Valentina DiMarco tomorrow, I'd like to go back to the crime scene," I say.

"I figured," Mitchell says. "We also need to check out Extreme Gymnastics. We've been focusing on Rebel, thinking the killer is one of Isabelle's rivals, but it's possible it's someone at Extreme."

"I'd hate to think it is Valentina," Mom says. I'm surprised she's allowing work talk at the dinner table, but I guess since it's affecting my eyesight, she's making an exception.

"So would I," I say.

"Have your senses hit on anything else, pumpkin?" Dad asks.

"Yeah. Today at Rebel's gym, my senses said 'balance beam.'"

"Did you read it while you were there?"

"I did. And I saw Phoebe Billings trying to convince

Tessa Harris to find out Valentina DiMarco's routine on the beam. Tessa refused and said it was cheating."

"Hmm." Dad pauses, and I know he's onto something. "The balance beam was Phoebe Billings best event, but she could never beat Isabelle on it. No one could."

"Did she beat Skylar Harris on beam?" I ask.

"Yes. It was the only event she beat Skylar on."

"Then that's not the event I saw in my first vision of the three of them." Why doesn't this add up?

"Maybe you were just supposed to see Phoebe's motive for wanting to beat Isabelle," Mitchell suggests around the food in his mouth.

"Swallow first. Then talk," I tell him. "This is all connected somehow. We're just not seeing it."

Mitchell places his hand on my leg. "Try using your other senses. You're getting really good at compensating. Maybe this isn't something we're meant to see."

"I don't have enough to go on yet. Sorry."

"Don't apologize. You know I wish I could..." He pauses, and then he takes my hand in his.

I feel his vulnerability. "Mitchell?" I ask.

"Mom, I know Piper told you about my mother."

Oh my goodness. He's going to talk to my parents about this. He's going to share his secret with them. "Mitchell, you don't have to."

"I know. I want to. They should know, and they should hear it from me." He clears his throat.

"Take your time, sweetie," Mom says. "We love you, and we're here for you."

"My mom was psychic, and it scared her more than anything. She foresaw her own death and thought she couldn't stop it. She was worried if she tried to something awful would happen to my brother and me. Like repercussions for messing with fate." He takes a few deep breaths before continuing. "I envy how well Piper handles her abilities, and I've always wished I had some myself."

"You have great intuition, Mitchell," I say.

"Thank you." He squeezes my hand. "I think my mom would have loved you, Piper. I think about these dinners, and I can see her sitting here with us, trying to solve cases or just talking about everyday things."

"I would have liked that," I say.

"I used to wonder why Nick and I never got our mom's abilities, but now I think my mom was meant to prepare me for Piper. For being there for Piper. For being the man she needs me to be."

Mom sniffles beside me. "Mitchell, your mother would be so proud of the man you've become."

"That's thanks to Piper, too. She helped me find myself when I was truly lost. And I'm going to do everything I can to help her get her sight back."

I don't think there's anything Mitchell can do, but I lean toward him and rest my head on his shoulder. "I know you will."

"So tell me what you need," Mitchell says.

I take a deep breath. I think I've known for a while now what I need to do. I've just been too scared to do it. "I need to fully step into Isabelle's shoes. I believe that's why I lost my sight. I have to experience the world the way she does. If I can do that, I think I'll find her killer."

"And how do you plan to do that, pumpkin?" Dad asks.

"I need to get the DiMarcos' permission to stay in Isabelle's apartment and have access to all her belongings."

"I can't imagine them liking that very much, even if it is to help find their daughter's killer," Mom says. "Not when you're questioning their other daughter for the murder."

"I know. It's not going to be easy, but I need to retrace Isabelle's footsteps." Hopefully not so closely that it puts my life in danger.

"I'll be there every step of the way," Mitchell says.

"Do you want us to keep Jezebel until you're finished?" Dad asks.

"Would you mind? She's very uneasy around me right now. I think she'd be happier and more herself here. She's so comfortable with you guys and Max."

Mom reaches for my hand. "Of course, sweetie."

Even though it's my right hand she's touching, I'm able to not read her. I smile.

"What?" Mitchell asks.

"Look." I lower my head to our hands even though I can't physically see them. "I'm not reading her."

"Do you think it's because you don't have all your senses?" Dad asks.

"I don't know. Or maybe I'm finally learning to control this."

————

I wake up Wednesday morning to the smell of coffee brewing. I sit up and throw the covers off me. It's little things that annoy me the most, like not being able to check the time without asking my phone to tell me. I guess I should be happy for that feature. I make my way to the bathroom to brush my teeth before I get dressed for the day. Thankfully, I'm not all that big on makeup because I'm not sure what would happen if I had to ask Mitchell to do my makeup for me.

"Hey, you're up," Mitchell says, walking into the bedroom as I finish getting dressed.

"Where were you?" I ask.

"I got a phone call and took it out in the hallway so I wouldn't wake you. How did you sleep?"

"I missed Jez. I never thought I would miss the cover hog, but I did."

He steps forward and presses a kiss to my forehead. "She'll be home soon. Life will be back to normal before we know it."

I hope so. "What was your phone call about?" I run a

brush through my hair to tame the bedhead I usually wake up with.

"It was Officer Gilbert. He let me know that Valentina DiMarco's lawyer arrived at the station about ten minutes ago. Valentina and her parents should be there shortly."

"Great, then we should get going."

"I also called your dad. He's setting up a meeting for us with Paige Rudolph. She's a coach at Extreme Gymnastics, and she was close with Isabelle."

"Also good. I want to check out any coaches and athletes who knew Isabelle and Valentina."

"I'll pour us some coffees to-go." Mitchell walks out of the room.

I try to remember where I put my purse yesterday. I know my phone is on the nightstand, so I grab that and then start searching the dresser for my purse. No luck. I step out into the living room. "Have you seen my purse?"

"It's on the kitchen counter," Mitchell says.

I almost bump into the end table beside the couch on the way. "What are the odds I wake up totally normal tomorrow?"

"Not good." Mitchell wraps an arm around me. "You're Piper Ashwell. You're far from normal, and that's what I love about you."

I roll my eyes. "You know what I mean. Caffeinate me." I hold out my hand, and Mitchell places a to-go mug into it. I take a sip. We keep toasted almond coffee on hand from Marcia's Nook. I don't know why, but it still tastes better when Marcia makes it. "Thank you. I needed that."

"Want to grab some food on the way to the station or wait until after we talk to the DiMarcos?"

I always want to eat, but I have a feeling we're short on time. "I overslept, didn't I?"

"Maybe, but I figured you could use the rest. We'll make it in plenty of time."

"Still, we better not keep them waiting. We can eat afterward."

The station is pretty empty when we arrive. Only Officer Gilbert and Chief Johansen are around. At least, those are the only two people's energies I can sense. "Where is everyone this morning?"

"How did you know they weren't here?" Mitchell asks.

"Easy. I can sense their energy."

"You're tuning in more lately, aren't you?"

"I kind of have to, or I'll wind up making a complete fool out of myself, and we both know that's your job."

"Absolutely. Don't go trying to steal my thunder." He places his hand on the small of my back and leads me to the interrogation room.

"Piper," Officer Gilbert says before I enter the room.

"Yes?"

"I let the lawyer know about your current condition. You know, with your eyesight." Officer Gilbert is young and tries too hard to be helpful sometimes, but his heart is always in the right place.

"Thank you. I appreciate it."

"No problem. If there's anything I can do to help, let me know. I love working with you."

"If we need another hand, I'll be sure to request you," I say.

"You can't see it, but I'm smiling."

I laugh. "I kind of figured as much."

"You coming?" Mitchell asks me.

"Yeah." I raise a hand to wave to Officer Gilbert before I allow Mitchell to bring me into the interrogation room. "Sorry for the delay," I say.

"No worries," says a voice I don't recognize. "I'm Brian Clark. I'll be representing Valentina."

"Good morning, Mr. Clark." There's a lot of apprehension in the room, and I know where it's coming from. "Valentina, I'm sure you're nervous right now, so I appreciate you coming in to speak with Detective Brennan and me again."

"Ms. Ashwell, I've advised my client not to speak without my approval, but she is nodding to acknowledge your comment," Mr. Clark says.

Mitchell pulls out a chair for me. "Maybe I can put everyone's minds at ease. I have a top suspect in this case, and that individual is not in this room."

"Oh, thank goodness," Mrs. DiMarco says.

"I need you to understand that Valentina's prints on the murder weapon are the reason we're here."

"But I already explained that," she says.

"Miss DiMarco," Mr. Clark says, cutting her off before she can say more.

"I think I can be of some help here," I say. "Valentina, I have a special gift called psychometry. I can touch your hand and know whether or not you're innocent. I already believe you are. Your energy right now is telling me you didn't hurt your sister. You feel extreme guilt for the relationship you had with her after the accident. You said some things that you know will make you look bad, and you're worried about that."

"Hold on," Mr. Clark says. "This is pure speculation."

"No, it's not, but I understand that you believe it is. Valentina knows I'm right, and that's all I care about right now." I turn my head back to the spot where Valentina's energy is coming from. "I believe you. Please let me help convince the others at this station that you're innocent."

"How?" she asks.

"I'm not sure I like this," Mr. DiMarco says.

"Piper has helped the WPD many times using her psychic abilities. I've seen her clear suspects this exact way. If you really want to put an end to this questioning, this is your best bet. If Valentina is innocent, Piper will see that."

"And this will all end?" Mrs. DiMarco asks.

"Yes," I say. "I promise."

"Mom, Dad, I want to do it," Valentina says.

"I can't advise this," Mr. Clark says.

THERE'S MORE THAN ONE WAY TO SENSE A KILLER

"He wouldn't," I say. "It's going to cost him a good chunk of his paycheck when you don't need his services."

"Valentina, you're sure about this?" her father asks.

It's quiet for a moment.

"She's nodding," Mitchell tells me.

I extend my right hand. "When you're ready, just place your hand in mine."

It takes her about thirty seconds to do so, but then I wrap my fingers around hers.

"Help!" Valentina screams from a dark trunk. "Somebody help me!" Her hands are zip-tied, but she laces her fingers together and pounds her fists on the trunk as the car begins to move.

I let go of her. "Mitchell, it's not her. She's the next victim."

CHAPTER TEN

Okay, so my people skills still need a lot of work. Blurting out that the DiMarco's second daughter is about to meet a similar fate to their recently murdered oldest daughter was pretty bad. Mrs. DiMarco is shrieking, Valentina is crying, and Mr. DiMarco is demanding police protection.

"Everyone calm down," Mitchell says in a loud voice. "Piper, I'd like to talk to you in private for a moment."

"No, I want to hear what she saw," Mrs. DiMarco says. "Please. I already lost one daughter. I can't lose another. You have to help us."

"Mitchell, they're right. They need to know," I say.

"She's only a kid, Piper." Mitchell places his hand on my leg, silently pleading with me to go easy on this girl and not blurt out what I saw.

"I think whoever killed Isabelle is going to kidnap

Valentina. That's what I saw. She was trying to free herself..." I stop and lower my head. I can't see their expressions, but I can feel their penetrating gazes and the overwhelming worry between them.

"Free myself from what?" Valentina asks.

"I'm not sure that's important," Mitchell says. "We need to get an officer stationed with Valentina at all times. I'll put Officer Gilbert on your house now. Valentina should remain there."

"I can't. I have to practice. The upcoming meet is too important to miss." Valentina sounds heartbroken.

"I thought you weren't even sure if you wanted to compete anymore," I say.

"Izzy trained me for this. I owe it to her to see this meet through. After that, I don't know what I'll do, but I'm going to compete in this meet for her."

"All right. Then I'll need to station one officer at your home and another to remain with Valentina at all times."

"Detective O'Reilly," I say. "She's a female, so she can go everywhere with Valentina, even the restroom."

"She's not cleared for fieldwork yet," Mitchell says. "I don't trust her to be able to protect Valentina if things get..." He pauses, realizing he shouldn't talk about how bad things could get with Valentina already so upset.

"Detective Brennan is right," I say. "Detective O'Reilly is recovering from a gunshot wound. She has limited mobility."

"Who else do you have?" Mr. DiMarco asks.

"What about you?" Valentina asks.

"Who?" I say. "Detective Brennan?"

"No, you."

"I'm afraid I need Piper to help me solve your sister's murder. She finds the best leads thanks to her special talents."

"Plus, she's blind, Valentina," Mrs. DiMarco says. "How would she protect you?"

"She makes me feel safe," Valentina says.

I realize I'm trying to project feelings of serenity at Valentina. I've never done that before. I want to help her, though. She just lost her sister, and she must be so scared right now finding out she's the next target.

"Stay put. I need to give this some thought," Mitchell says. "Piper, we need to devise a plan." His chair slides back, making a scraping sound on the floor.

I stand up. "Your lawyer isn't going to dismiss himself because you're paying him by the hour," I say before letting Mitchell lead me out.

"What were you doing back there?"

"I don't know. First, I saw the future, which is still baffling to me." My visions of the future don't usually come that easily. "Then I somehow was able to pick up on Valentina's emotions and calm them with my own energy. I can't explain it." I've never done anything like this before, and I can't even figure out how it happened.

"Okay, what are we dealing with here? This kidnapper, why would they take Valentina? Are they after a ransom? That doesn't seem to fit with Isabelle's murder in any way."

"No, it doesn't. If someone wanted a ransom, it would make more sense to kidnap Tessa Harris. Her family is loaded."

"Exactly, so it can't be about the money."

Revenge.

"My senses say this is about revenge."

"Revenge for what, though? What does harming the DiMarco sisters avenge?"

I don't know. We haven't even looked into who might not like Valentina. We've been focusing solely on Isabelle. "Wait." I hold up a hand. "Phoebe Billings. She hated Isabelle, and the vision I had of Phoebe and Tessa was about getting Valentina's balance beam routine."

"So you think it's Phoebe," Mitchell says.

"Did you ever question if Valentina and Phoebe were working together?" Detective O'Reilly says, coming up behind me again. I don't like that she's making that a habit.

"When did you get here?" Mitchell asks her.

"About five minutes ago. I'm telling you it's clearly Phoebe Billings and Valentina DiMarco who killed Isabelle DiMarco. All the evidence points to them being in on it together."

"What evidence?" I ask. Detective O'Reilly is about 'seeing is believing,' so what did she see that we didn't?

"First, the murder weapon. Valentina's prints are all

over it. Why? Because she had a convenient excuse for it if the police discovered it was, in fact, the murder weapon. But first she moved it to try to keep the police from finding it."

"Did you just speculate?" I ask. She never does that. She criticizes others for doing it.

"No. I made an educated guess based on factual evidence."

"You speculated," I repeat. "Dare I say I'm rubbing off on you?"

"Phoebe flipped out on you at the gym, right?" she continues, ignoring my comment.

"Correct."

"That means she's hiding something, something she thinks you know."

"There could be other reasons she'd flip out, but in this case, I do agree with you, so go on." I cross my arms and cock my head at where I sense her energy is coming from. "Are you waving your hand in the air?" I ask her.

"Can you see me?"

"No, I feel shifts in your energy."

"She's frowning," Mitchell says. "Not that you couldn't guess that."

Her reactions to my psychic abilities are as easy to guess as my reactions to Mitchell's stupid sayings.

"I've watched tapes of Phoebe's competitions with Isabelle. She clearly hated her. In fact, in one tape, she threatened Isabelle."

"When?" Mitchell asks.

"It was about a month ago. I'm surprised you haven't watched it."

"Some of us are actually out in the field doing real police work instead of sitting at a desk for not following rules," Mitchell says.

"Didn't you just come off of a two-week suspension?" she asks, shocking me. She usually looks for Mitchell's approval. I've never seen her go at him hard like this. She must really hate being assigned desk duty.

"Is there a problem here?" Chief Johansen asks.

"No, Chief," Detective O'Reilly says immediately.

"I sure hope not. O'Reilly, isn't there a desk you should be sitting behind?"

Her mood shifts. "Yes, Chief." She walks away, her footfalls clicking against the floor.

"The killer had soft footsteps," I say. "That could definitely point to it being a gymnast."

"Which could incriminate either girl, but Valentina can't kidnap herself," Mitchell says.

"No, especially since the person who kidnaps her puts her in the trunk of a car and drives off," I say.

"Did you have a vision?" Chief Johansen asks me.

"Yes. Chief, we need constant police protection on Valentina DiMarco, or she will wind up being a second victim."

"Okay. Let me see who I can assign to that."

"Officer Gilbert really wants to help with this case," I say.

Chief Johansen scoffs. "Gilbert wants his hand in everything."

"Except discovering bodies at crime scenes," Mitchell says. "The guy is kind of squeamish around dead people."

And unfortunately for Officer Gilbert, he's come across several recently.

The door to the interrogation room opens. "Good luck with them," Brian Clark says. "They just told me my services are no longer needed, so they're all yours."

"Sorry about that," I say, but truthfully, I'm not sorry at all. He wasn't going to help the DiMarcos. He just wanted an easy paycheck.

"Let's talk to Phoebe Billings," Mitchell says once Brian Clark leaves and Chief Johansen retreats to his office.

"What doesn't make sense to me is how Phoebe can be the guilty party if she's in police custody. She can't kidnap Valentina."

"We don't know that for sure. We aren't holding her for murder. She's here on assault charges. She'll pay a fine and get out of here. How immediate did your vision feel?"

"I'm not sure. Isn't there anything else you can pin on her?"

"Honestly, our best bet is to interrogate her and see if we can get something out of her that will prove she's guilty."

I don't like our odds. I've broken criminals before and gotten them to confess, but Phoebe doesn't seem like the type.

It takes about twenty minutes to get Phoebe upstairs and into an interrogation room, and I couldn't be more surprised when Phoebe's lawyer says, "Long time no see."

"Why would you hire Brian Clark?" I ask Phoebe, recognizing the voice of the man I convinced the DiMarcos to fire. "He was just here representing Valentina DiMarco."

"Valentina didn't need my services anymore, and Ms. Billings does."

"You pounced right on that, didn't you?" I ask.

"I felt I could be of service to Ms. Billings, so I did what any lawyer would do in my position."

"I'm not sure other lawyers would be happy about you making it sound as though they're all like you." I cross my arms in my seat. I sense Phoebe's energy coming from across the table. She's confused and angry.

"You better not be playing me and still secretly working for the DiMarcos," Phoebe says. "First, I get some stupid public defender, and now you. I swear the universe is out to get me."

I can tell she really does feel that way. I lean closer to her. "You thought Isabelle had everything handed to her. And Skylar, too. You hated them because you had to work twice as hard as they did, and you didn't have nearly as much."

"Who have you been talking to? Did you call my mother?" She sounds appalled at that notion.

"No. I'm piecing together what I know and trying to see it from your point of view."

"Last time I checked, you can't see anything." Phoebe scoffs.

"You do realize Piper is trying to help you," Mitchell says. "I, on the other hand, think you killed Isabelle DiMarco and are planning to harm Valentina DiMarco next. My only question is why."

To win.

"You want to win. You're tired of losing to the DiMarco sisters," I say.

"News flash. I don't compete anymore. And what you said about killing Isabelle isn't true. I'm not admitting to anything."

"Your lawyer should be telling you not to admit to anything, but notice how quiet he's become. How can you afford him? How did your parents afford to send you to Rebel to train for all those years?" Phoebe's life and her personality are starting to make sense to me now.

"You don't have to answer that," Mr. Clark finally says. "My client is here for assault charges. Let's keep the questions to that."

"No, at the moment, she's here to answer questions about Isabelle DiMarco's murder," Mitchell says.

"The balance beam was your best event," I say.

"Yeah, I was practically unbeatable." Her energy shifts, and I get the distinct feeling she's both leaning and looking away from me.

"Except for Isabelle," I say. "That must have been hard. You mentioned your mother earlier. Did she raise you alone?"

"I knew you talked to her. I can't believe she spilled my life story to you. Let me guess. She said she'd tell you whatever you needed to know if it would help me. Everything she did had that label attached: 'to help Phoebe.'" She huffs. "It was her go-to excuse. She worked long hours to help me. She did favors for—" Phoebe stops talking.

"Favors for whom?" Mitchell asks.

"It's not important," Phoebe says, but I can tell it is.

Samuel Rebel.

I press my hand to my mouth.

"Piper, what is it?" Mitchell asks.

"That's how your mother paid for your gymnastics training."

"Shut up. You have no idea what you're talking about."

"What is she talking about?" Mr. Clark asks. "I'd like a word with my client."

"Why?" Phoebe asks. "My mother already told her. That much is obvious. We don't need to discuss my mother's indiscretions."

"You didn't know at the time, did you?" I ask.

"Know what?" Mitchell asks.

"That Phoebe's mother didn't pay for her training in money. She did other favors for Samuel Rebel."

"I said shut up!" Phoebe's chair slides back across the floor, and her energy comes rushing right at me. Sounds of her on top of the table are my cue to back away before she assaults me.

CHAPTER ELEVEN

There's a scuffle. Like a slamming of a body on the table and a whoosh of air from Phoebe's lungs. Then there's a grunt and the metallic click of handcuffs.

"Get your hands off my client," Mr. Clark says.

"Not a chance. She's going back to the holding cell. This isn't the first time she's tried to assault Piper. You're well aware of that."

She tried to hit me again. But why would her mother's —I'm going to think of it as an affair because even though that still sounds awful it's not quite as disgusting as prostitution—make Phoebe so defensive now. She doesn't seem like she even has a relationship with her mother anymore. There has to be another reason Phoebe is so upset.

Isabelle.

"Isabelle knew?" I ask, raising my head but not exactly sure where Phoebe is in the room anymore because the emotions and energy in the small space are all over the place now.

It gets quiet. Phoebe's lack of protest tells me I'm right. Or my senses are, at least, since they told me.

"Isabelle found out about your mom and Samuel Rebel."

"Is that what drove you to kill her?" Mitchell asks.

"Do not answer that," Mr. Clark says. "I insist you let me confer with my client in private."

"Fine," Mitchell says, and then his hand slips into mine.

I stand up and allow him to lead me to the door. Finding my way on my own amidst the chaos in this room would be impossible.

As soon as we step out of the interrogation room and the door closes behind us, Mitchell says, "How did you get all that? It was like you really did talk to Phoebe's mother."

"It all sort of just came to me."

"Your senses clued you in on that much all at once?"

"Kind of. It started with me reading the energy Phoebe was projecting. It's almost like her energy screams at you."

"Much like the rest of her. You need to press charges against her. It's the only way we can keep her here for now."

He's right. We can't let Phoebe go, or Valentina's life will be in danger. My vision of the future can be changed. That's what makes seeing the future so tricky. It's never set in stone. It can change. The problem is identifying the right things to alter to make it change. If Phoebe is the killer, keeping her detained will prevent Valentina's kidnapping, but if we're wrong...

"Simple assault will only get her a year or two in prison and a fine of about five grand," Mitchell says. "She's tried to assault you multiple times now, though, so we might be able to go with aggravated assault. It could be tough though since Phoebe didn't attack you with a weapon. We might not be able to prove she meant to cause you serious bodily injury. If we do though, she'd get up to twenty years and fined up to twenty-five grand."

"We both know the aggravated assault charges won't stick. Besides, we just need her detained."

"I think a restraining order would be good as well. I can also play the angle that you're consulting with the WPD, so it was like assaulting an officer of the law."

"Mitchell, stop." He's losing sight of what's really important right now because he's worried about my safety.

He reaches for my arm. "Sorry, but it's hard to watch someone try to hurt you twice and do nothing about it."

"I get that, but right now it's Valentina DiMarco's life in danger, not mine."

"We don't know that for sure. If Phoebe is the killer, she might come after you now that you've outed her secrets like that. How were you able to sense so much, anyway?"

"I don't know. Maybe my senses are taking pity on me because I can't see."

"Well, it's really incredible. I know I keep saying that, but I can't get over how well you're doing."

"Isabelle found out about Phoebe's mom and Samuel Rebel," I say, "but it doesn't make sense that she'd only found out recently."

"That's true. Phoebe doesn't compete anymore, and I doubt her mother is still involved with Rebel. It didn't seem like Phoebe really communicates much with her mother these days either."

"No, it doesn't, which means that Phoebe probably held a grudge against Isabelle for years. This is why she hated her. Not only for besting her on the balance beam but for knowing her darkest secret." I will my senses to pick up on something else.

"Why wouldn't Phoebe go after Isabelle back then?" Mitchell asks.

"I don't know. Maybe she planned to, but something stopped her."

Accident.

"The accident stopped her?" I ask aloud.

"You mean Isabelle's car accident? It made it so she couldn't compete anymore. I guess Phoebe wouldn't see Isabelle as a threat to her after that."

"Yeah, maybe."

"But that's not what you meant?" he asks.

"I don't know. The word accident came from my senses."

"Again? Piper, I've never seen you this in tune with them."

"Yeah, it's kind of weird. Like this voice in my head that keeps chirping."

"Come here." He takes my arm and leads me to a chair. I can sense Mitchell's energy on the objects around me, so I know we're at his desk. "Do you think it's possible your senses try to tell you this much all the time but you aren't as tuned in to them?"

"You think I'm tuning in more now because I can't see."

He's quiet for a second. "Sorry, I just nodded out of habit. Yes, that's what I think."

It doesn't feel right to me. "I don't think so. I think my abilities are picking up the slack for me and helping more than they typically would."

"Then you think this is temporary."

This time I'm the one who nods. It would be nice to have answers come to me this often all the time. I'd probably solve cases much quicker. "I guess I need to enjoy the heightened abilities as long as I can."

Accident.

"Yes, I'm aware. The accident stopped Isabelle from competing and probably saved her from Phoebe's wrath."

No.

"No? What do you mean no? You just told me that's what happened. You can't take it back now."

"Um, Piper," Mitchell whispers. "You're arguing with yourself, and while I'm sort of used to this, Detective O'Reilly is staring at you from her desk." He raises his voice. "Problem, O'Reilly? You look like you're straining your back to lean this way and eavesdrop."

"Let her be. She doesn't understand me. If she's watching, it might mean she's actually trying to."

"Doubtful. You cut her too much slack, Piper."

"She saved my life, Mitchell."

"You wouldn't have needed to be saved if not for her carelessness. She protected you to save her own career after she messed up. Don't give her any credit for the way things went down on that case."

I reach forward and place my hand on his. "Breathe. I'm fine."

"Sorry." I can feel him trying to control his emotions for my sake. Mitchell is one of those people, like Phoebe Billings, who projects their feelings outward. It can help me or totally overwhelm me depending on the situation. "Better?" he asks after taking several deep, calming breaths.

"Yes, thank you."

He doesn't let go of my hand. "What were your senses saying?"

"They said the accident didn't save Isabelle from Phoebe's wrath. I think."

"That could be because Phoebe wound up killing her seven years later."

I've been wrong in my interpretations of my senses before. Getting verbal responses might seem straightforward, but it's not. Especially when my senses say no to something because I never know exactly what they're saying no to. Does it mean that the accident didn't save Isabelle? That Phoebe's wrath didn't end there?

Not an accident.

"Whoa!"

"What?" Mitchell holds my hand in both of his.

"I got more just now when I was trying to work through this in my head, and it's pretty crazy."

"How so?"

"My senses told me the accident wasn't an accident."

"That's impossible, Piper."

I pull my hand away and cock my head. "You know better than that." My senses are never wrong. Not when they flat-out tell me something.

"Okay, let's figure this out then because it's not adding up at all. I'm going to pull up the accident report from seven years ago. Give me a minute." He lets go of my hand, and the sound of his keyboard tells me he's looking into the computer system.

I lean back in my chair. How can a car accident not be an accident? Did the driver hit Isabelle on purpose? Did he intend to kill her? Did Phoebe know the driver?

Of course, now my senses choose to be silent. Thanks a lot.

"What are you rolling your eyes at?" Mitchell asks. "I'm pretty sure I haven't done anything to annoy you in the last thirty seconds."

I smirk. "No. It's my senses. I was coming up with theories in my head, and I'm not getting any response whatsoever."

"Ah. Well, maybe that means you're on the right track, and your senses don't want to butt in."

"Maybe." And maybe not. Being psychic is tricky sometimes. Or most of the time, really.

"All right. According to the accident report, Chad Hooper is the truck driver who hit Isabelle. He claimed something hit his windshield, causing him to swerve."

"Something like what?" I ask. "A bird?"

"He didn't know what it was. The police found a bullet lodged in the road, though. They said a hunter could have been too close to the road and shot into the traffic. They questioned a hunter named Ruben Ballock, who was in the area at the time. They couldn't prove anything, though. While the type of bullets matched what he was using, they couldn't prove it came from his gun."

"I want to talk to Chad Hooper," I say. "I can read him and see the accident."

"Piper, last time you saw that accident, you lost your eyesight."

"Yeah, but this time I should be able to see it from

Chad Hooper's perspective. And besides, I already lost my eyesight. It's not like I can lose it again."

"What about Phoebe Billings?" he asks.

"She's not going anywhere, right?"

"Good point." His keys click again, and I assume he's finding contact information for Chad Hooper. "Okay, Chad still lives in town. I've got an address."

The odds of him being home on a Wednesday aren't good. "Can you find his current place of employment?" I ask. I doubt he works for the truck company anymore. Who would be able to after an accident like that?

"Your dad might be better suited to finding that for us. We can call him on the way. I'd like to check out Chad Hooper's residence even if he isn't home."

He doesn't say it, but he knows I could possibly read something there without even talking to Chad. "I like the way you think."

"Hopefully, you like more than just that about me. I am your husband after all."

"Stop fishing for compliments. We have work to do."

Mitchell calls Dad on the drive, and we get him to work finding Chad Hooper's current place of employment. Mitchell slows the car. "This is odd."

"What?"

"Well, the house looks like an old garage."

"You mean it was converted into a living space like Isabelle DiMarco's family did for her?" What a coincidence that would be.

"No. It looks like there used to be a house on the property, but it's gone now. All that's left is the garage, which has seen better days." Mitchell parks and cuts the engine.

What if Chad Hooper lost everything because of the accident? "Did the DiMarco family sue?" I ask Mitchell.

"Yes, for reckless driving. Chad's claim that something hit his windshield couldn't be verified because the entire windshield shattered in the collision. There was no proof of anything."

"Then how did a lawsuit hold up if it was ruled an accident?"

"It was determined that Chad was speeding. I think he had a bad lawyer who settled to avoid the ruling of an accident being overturned. Chad pled guilty to the speeding charge."

"Was the lawyer Brian Clark?" I ask.

Yes.

"Oh my goodness. Mitchell I was kidding, but I'm right. Brian Clark has been all over this, and I think it's intentional."

"You don't think everything traces back to him, do you?"

"I don't know. But why would the DiMarcos hire him to represent Valentina if he's the lawyer who represented the man who hit Isabelle?" They had to have known.

"Piper, what if the DiMarco family isn't as innocent in all this as we've been assuming."

I turn toward him in my seat. I might not be able to see his face, but I picture it in my mind. "Go on."

"Okay, I might be reaching here, but what if the DiMarcos hired Brian Clark seven years ago to represent Chad Hooper."

I'm about to tell him how that makes zero sense, but then what he's getting at comes to me. "You think they hired him to sabotage Chad Hooper's case?"

"Isn't it possible? They pay him to convince Chad to plead guilty to speeding. Clark gets paid by both clients, and the DiMarcos make out with a lawsuit payout."

"If that's true, it would explain why Brian Clark is so eager to be part of anything related to Isabelle DiMarco now. He needs to make sure the truth about seven years ago never comes to the surface." He's trying to protect himself and his career. I knew he was a dirty lawyer. The only person he wants to help is himself.

"So he represents Valentina to make sure the family is keeping up their end of the deal. Then he represents Phoebe Billings so he can be in on the questioning and find out what we know."

"Yes, which is why he was so quiet during the interrogations. He wasn't really there to represent either girl. He was there to find out if we knew anything about Isabelle's accident. He must have questioned if we'd open that case back up now that Isabelle was murdered." But what made him think we'd question the accident? It's been seven years.

"You want to go see if Chad is home?" Mitchell asks me.

"Might as well." I open my door and step out. Mitchell meets me.

"The driveway is overgrown with weeds, so be careful."

"Is there anything left to indicate a house was ever here?" I ask.

"Um, I think we need to get closer to see." He brings me to the end of the driveway, or that's what it feels like under my feet. I can make out the subtle variations in the terrain. There's no gravel left here at all. "Okay," Mitchell says, "I see remnants of a foundation, but it looks like the place was cleared out pretty well. There's not much left."

I bend down and reach for the ground. Mitchell moves my hand, guiding it by my wrist since it's my right hand, and he doesn't want to interfere with me trying to read the rubble. My fingers touch a bit of concrete.

An image fills my head.

The house is white with black shutters. It's a bi-level with three steps leading to the front door, which is a bright red.

Then the image shifts.

The shutters hang off the siding. The front porch steps have collapsed completely, and the front door has a condemned notice on it.

"The house literally fell apart."

"Probably because all of Chad Hooper's money went

to paying that lawsuit," Mitchell says, guiding me as I stand up. "Did you sense Chad at all?"

"No. I only saw the house before and after Chad lost his money."

"Losing his home would be motive for murdering Isabelle DiMarco," Mitchell says.

"I thought you were convinced Phoebe Billings is the killer."

"Oh, I'm not saying she's not. She's still my prime suspect, but I can see how going from a nice home to living in a tiny garage would make the man angry."

"Let's see if he's home," I say.

Mitchell walks me over to the garage and knocks. "We're at the side door," he tells me.

I figured as much. It would be weird to knock on the giant door on the front of the garage. We wait a few minutes, and Mitchell tries knocking again, but no one answers.

"Let me," I say, reaching for the doorknob. My fingers wrap around the metal.

A man unlocks the door, but instead of going inside the garage, he turns to look at where his house used to stand. "Someone should pay for this. I'm a victim, too, but no one cared about the middle-age man who lost everything. Only the poor teenager who can't see. Well, I wish I couldn't see what a mess my life has become because of this. It's about time someone paid for what's happened to me."

CHAPTER TWELVE

"Piper?" Mitchell waits patiently as I regain control of my own emotions.

"Chad believes he's a victim in all of this. He's angry, and he wanted someone to pay for what happened to him. He feels like his life was taken from him and no one cared."

"Then he definitely had resentment toward Isabelle and her family," Mitchell says.

"Yes, that's putting it mildly." We need Dad to hurry up with Chad Hooper's place of employment. "Can you call my dad?"

"You know he hates when we rush him, Piper."

"Chicken. Dial, and I'll talk to him."

He huffs, but he makes the call. "Dad, we're at Chad Hooper's house, or what's left of it. Piper had a vision and believes Hooper wanted revenge. Any chance you found where he's working?"

"He bounced around from job to job after the car accident. He was fired from the truck company. From there he worked as a garbage man for a while. Then he went to a recycling facility. After that it was a bowling alley. It seems like every time I find something, I also find out he was fired. I just got off the phone with the owner of the bowling alley. He didn't know where Chad went after he left there."

This isn't helpful. "What about his last tax return?" I ask.

"The odds that he's held the same job since January are slim to none, pumpkin. He doesn't tend to last longer than a month anywhere. The only job he held for years was at the trucking company."

Which implies he actually liked that job. More reason for him to hate Isabelle and her family. "Okay, Dad, keep looking. Mitchell and I will try something else in the meantime."

"I'll call you the second I have something," he says before ending the call.

"What exactly are we trying in the meantime?" Mitchell asks.

"We still haven't been to Extreme Gymnastics." Our trip there kept getting pushed off for more immediate concerns. "I say it's time we check it out. We can find out if anyone there knew Chad Hooper or saw him lurking around."

"Let's do it."

Driving has never been entirely safe for me, considering I never know what will trigger a vision. And being behind the wheel is probably one of the worst places for me when I have a vision. I'm a danger to myself and anyone else on the road. It's why Mitchell drives us almost everywhere. But I love my Mazda 6, and I miss it. It's been sitting in front of my office for days now. Poor car.

"What are you thinking?" Mitchell asks me.

"That I wish I was driving."

"My driving isn't that bad," he says, sounding offended.

I laugh. "It's not that. I miss being able to drive."

"Oh, that makes sense. Do you have any idea what kind of vision will reverse your blindness?"

I've been operating under the assumption that solving this case will restore my sight, but maybe it will take a vision to do it. "Are we cleared to have me stay in Isabelle's apartment tonight?" I ask.

"Yes. The family basically feels we're welcome to do what we need to do to solve Isabelle's murder and protect Valentina."

"Good. Maybe reading something else of Isabelle's will do the trick."

Mitchell slows the car to a stop. "We're here. It looks a lot like Rebel Gymnastics from the outside. I'm still a little surprised that Rebel was named after the gym's owner. I thought it was like Extreme and just a word to describe the gym's philosophy or something."

"Philosophy?" I ask, unclicking my seat belt. "*Rebel* and *extreme* are philosophies in your mind?"

"You know what I mean. Rebel is like the kids who break the rules, and the ones at Extreme push the limits."

"You're cute," I say.

"Did you just compliment me?" he asks, and I can hear the smile in his voice.

"Don't let it go to your head. It was a backhanded compliment. I was actually insulting your train of thought."

"Oh, I see. More of a 'I'm lucky I'm cute because I'm dumb' kind of thing."

"I'd never call you dumb. You're very smart, a great detective, and very intuitive whether you realize it or not. But you're also really corny at times."

"All I heard was compliments." He opens his door and hurries around the car to get mine in record time. "I even view being corny as a compliment," he says, taking my hand.

"Only you would," I say.

He stops me with a kiss before I can insult him further. "And you love me."

I push my palm against his chest. "We're on duty, Detective."

"Right." He loops my arm through his and brings me

to the door. "Paige Rudolph should be expecting us thanks to your dad calling her."

I almost forget Dad set up a meeting with her for us, and here I was thinking I came up with a plan to keep moving on the case while Dad searched for Chad Hooper. Really, this was our plan from the start. I just forgot.

When Mitchell opens the door, I can immediately sense a difference with this gym. Rebel was full of determination and pressure. Extreme is more laid back. And I also get a sense of worry.

"I'm sorry, but today's practice is closed. No spectators," a woman says.

"I'm Detective Brennan with the Weltunkin PD, and this is my partner, Piper Ashwell. We're here to see Paige Rudolph. She's expecting us," Mitchell says, and I have no doubt he's also flashing his badge.

"Oh, yes, Paige told me you were coming. Sorry for the confusion. I just assumed you two were a couple."

"Well, you didn't assume incorrectly. We're married," Mitchell says. I almost blush at the pride in his voice when he says it. Sometimes I don't think I deserve him. I'm not about to tell him that, though.

"Wow, married and partners on the job," she says. "That's impressive. I think I'd kill my boyfriend if I had to see him twenty-four seven."

"I know the feeling," I joke.

She laughs. "You're funny." She pauses, and I sense a

shift in her energy. "I hope you don't mind me asking, but are you vision impaired?"

"I am. It's a temporary condition."

"I only asked because one of our former coaches was blind. We have some provisions in place that helped her get around in here. For instance, there's an aisle down the center of the gym. It's widened to allow for easy passage with a walking stick if you use one."

"That would be him," I say, patting Mitchell's arm.

"Well, he's a very attractive walking stick. The nicest one I've seen. Don't tell my boyfriend I said that. And I'm not hitting on you or anything, Detective."

Mitchell laughs. "I didn't think you were, considering I just told you Piper and I are married."

"Right, well, I'll take you to Paige. She's over by the balance beam."

What is with the balance beam? I feel like every time Mitchell and I step foot inside a gym, I'm directed to the balance beam either because the person we came to see is there or my senses tell me to read it.

"You actually look like my boyfriend," the girl continues. "You have similar facial features."

"Aw, and here you thought you were one-of-a-kind," I tease him.

"Oh, sorry. I hope that didn't offend you," the girl says.

"No, you're fine," Mitchell assures her. "Piper just likes to make sure I don't get a big head."

"Your head looks perfect to me," the girl says.

I roll my eyes. Despite what she claims, she's definitely flirting with my husband. "Isn't it a blow to your ego when you openly flirt with someone and they don't acknowledge it?" I ask her.

"I'm sorry?" It comes out as a question, not an apology.

"You should be sorry. I might not be able to see you batting your eyes at my husband, but I am standing right here with him. You're being rude and completely inappropriate."

"She's right," Mitchell says. "Not only are you disrespecting my wife, but you're ignoring the fact that I, an officer of the law, already told you I'm not interested."

"Is there a problem, Savannah?" a man asks.

"No, sir. Everything is fine. These detectives are here to speak with Paige."

"I'll take it from here. You can return to your desk," he tells her.

Her footsteps hurry away, quickly but quietly. "She's a former gymnast," I say. "Her feet are very light on the ground." It reminds me a little of the killer in my vision.

"Yes, she is. Truth be told, she wasn't a very good gymnast. She's not a very good office worker either. I'm sorry for any trouble she might have caused you. I'm Xavier Shaw, owner of Extreme."

"Xavier, Extreme, I see what you did there," Mitchell says. "Clever."

"Yes, well, I didn't have a last name that suited the gym like my competitor." He laughs.

"Is there a rivalry between the two gyms?" I ask.

"Naturally. We both want to be the best gym. It's odd for two gyms to be in the same town."

But Weltunkin is a wealthy area for the most part. We've drawn some big athletes over the years, so it does make sense in that regard.

"What can you tell us about Isabelle DiMarco?" Mitchell asks.

"Isabelle." He sighs. "She was one of my favorites. So disciplined. This gym was her life. When her sight was taken from her, I cried. I knew she'd never be the same."

"Is that why you hired her as a coach?" I ask.

"No, it wasn't out of pity. Isabelle studied the sport so much she knew it inside and out. She was my best coach. The girls respected her and never questioned her training."

"What about Valentina?" I ask.

"She was the exception, but they were sisters. Siblings argue, so I think it was only normal that they had their issues."

"Detective Brennan?" comes a soft voice behind us.

"Ah, Paige. Are you finished working with Mandy and Mindy on beam?" Mr. Shaw asks.

"No, but Natalie is with them right now."

"Okay, well, I'll let you three talk. It was nice meeting you both." His footsteps are loud, definitely not those of a gymnast.

"We can talk in the back room," Paige says. "Follow me."

"You have gymnasts named Mindy and Mandy?" Mitchell asks.

"Yes, they're twins."

"Is Valentina here today?" I ask.

Paige slows to a stop. "Oh my goodness. I didn't realize."

I know she's referring to my lack of sight. "It's okay."

"I should have known. I was good friends with Isabelle. I should recognize the signs."

"It's really fine."

"Valentina called out today. Her parents said she'd be back tomorrow and mentioned something about a police escort."

"We believe it's in Valentina's best interest to be guarded by an officer at all times," Mitchell says.

"Why?" Paige asks. A door opens, and then a light flicks on in front of me. "Come in."

Mitchell and I step into the room.

"I can't really get into the details at this time," Mitchell says.

"Should I be worried about my safety here?" she asks.

"No," I say. "It's nothing like that." I don't get the sense that anyone other than Valentina is in danger. This is personal and has to do with the DiMarco family. "Detective Brennan, can you show Paige a photograph of Chad Hooper and see if she recognizes him?" I ask.

Mitchell keeps his elbow bent for me to hold on to as he fumbles with his phone. "Have you seen this man around the gym?" he asks Paige.

"No. I've never seen that man before. Why?"

"It's probably nothing. We're just being careful." Mitchell must return his phone to his pocket because his arm lowers at his side.

"What can you tell us about Isabelle?" Mitchell asks.

"She was an amazing coach. The girls really loved her."

"Was there any animosity between Isabelle and Phoebe Billings of Rebel Gymnastics?" Mitchell asks.

Paige gets quiet, and I can hear her swallow hard. "Phoebe is a hothead. Isabelle told me they competed against each other when they were growing up. Whenever Extreme and Rebel were at meets together, Phoebe would glare at Isabelle. She hated her. I didn't understand it because how can you not feel sorry for someone whose dream was completely destroyed by a freak accident? Isabelle could have been a legend. She was that good. And then it was all taken from her."

"Can I get you a tissue?" Mitchell asks her.

"No, I'm okay. I'm sorry I'm falling apart like this. Isabelle was my friend. I still can't believe she's gone."

"It sounds like she was very well liked around here," I say.

Paige inhales a shaky breath. It's barely audible, but I hear it all the same.

"Someone didn't like her?" I ask. "Someone at this gym?"

"Who are you looking for?" Mitchell asks. "She just looked through the windows behind us," Mitchell says for my benefit.

"I don't want to get anyone in trouble. It's nothing really."

"You're going to have to let us determine whether or not it's anything. Who didn't get along with Isabelle, Paige? I need a name."

Natalie Courtwright.

"Natalie Courtwright," I say. "She's the other coach. The one you told Mr. Shaw is training the twins while you talk to us."

"How did you know that?" Paige asks.

"That's not important. Tell us about Natalie and Isabelle," I say.

"It's not like they hated each other or anything. I swear." I feel a slight push of air in my direction. If I had to guess, I'd say Paige is holding up both hands in front of her. "Natalie thought she should be the head coach. She didn't understand how Mr. Shaw could give that position to Isabelle when she couldn't see. Honestly, Isabelle was the better coach, but I could see Natalie's perspective, too. At meets, Natalie handled all the paperwork and checking the athletes in. I thought maybe they should share the position of head coach."

"It didn't bother you that you weren't a head coach?" Mitchell asks.

"Me? No." She makes a small sound somewhere between a laugh and a sigh. "I love working with the girls, but I'm not head coach material." She's too timid. She lacks the authority a head coach needs.

"Did Natalie and Isabelle get into arguments a lot?" Mitchell asks.

"Kind of. It caused some tension. Natalie even sided with Valentina every time Isabelle got on Valentina's case about not trying hard enough. The tension in the gym got intense sometimes."

Yet it's not here now. Is that because Natalie got what she wanted? "Natalie is head coach now, isn't she?" I ask.

"Yes." Paige's voice is small.

Natalie got what she wanted. But what lengths did she go to in order to get it?

CHAPTER THIRTEEN

Natalie might have gotten along with Valentina before because it was in her best interest to do so, but now that Natalie is head coach, would she have a motive to kidnap Valentina? I can't see a reason for it, but I don't know much of anything about Natalie. I need to talk to her.

"Paige, you've been very helpful. Thank you," I say. "I think we should talk to Natalie."

"Oh, no. Please don't." Paige reaches for my hand.

"Just keep your mouth shut, Paige," Natalie says.

"But you're going to ruin Valentina's chances of a good score. That routine isn't nearly complicated enough."

"I'm the head coach now. I get to make that decision, not you."

"What happened?" Paige asks.

Mitchell has his arms around me as if holding me up. "I think Piper just got a little dizzy. I'll take care of her.

You're free to go, Paige. Thank you again for speaking with us."

The door opens and closes.

"What did you see?" Mitchell asks, letting go of me now that we're alone.

"Natalie threatening Paige. What did I do? Why did Paige react that way?"

"You yanked your hand away from her like she was going to hit you."

"I was Paige in my vision. She was afraid of Natalie Courtwright. She thought Natalie was sabotaging Valentina's routine on the balance beam. She said Valentina wouldn't be able to score high enough to win with that routine. Natalie didn't like being questioned, and she made that clear."

"The routines are scored based on difficulty, so if Natalie gave Valentina an easier routine, it would affect the team's overall score."

"Are you questioning if Natalie is somehow trying to sabotage Extreme at the upcoming meet?" Could someone at Rebel Gymnastics be paying her off? Phoebe maybe?

"I know you're thinking the same thing I am," Mitchell says. "Natalie and Phoebe might be in on this together."

"Which means Valentina isn't safe, even with Phoebe in police custody."

"Officer Gilbert is with Valentina now. Officer Lewalski will take over for him this evening."

I still think it should be a female officer guarding Valentina, but it's not my call. "We need evidence."

"Nothing new there."

"I also want to read the balance beam and talk to Natalie Courtwright."

"I think you should read the beam first. You might find out something and get Natalie to admit to it." He's clearly worried we won't get the evidence we need.

"Okay. Why don't you start questioning Natalie while I read the balance beam?"

"I don't know how to put this delicately so you don't get offended," Mitchell says.

"You don't trust me without you by my side since I can't see." I cross my arms. "This place made provisions for Isabelle's blindness. I'll be fine."

"Yes, but she worked here every day. She knew the layout. You don't."

I hate when he's logical at my expense. "Then tell me the layout. Describe it to me. You said there are windows in here, right?"

"Yes, but I'd be guessing how far apart things are. I'm not as good as you are at judging distance."

Because he hasn't spent his life tuning out the world by counting the steps between objects the way I have.

"Do your best. We have to make this work."

He takes two steps away from me. "Okay, there's a straight path from this room to the front of the gym."

I already knew that since it's the way we got here.

146

"About twenty feet on the left is the parallel bars. Beyond that is the balance beam."

"Is it centrally located?" I ask.

"Yes. The other side has the vault. There's a long mat so they can run—"

"Focus on the balance beam. I don't need to know about the rest."

"Right. Natalie is off to the side of the beam, so I can walk you that far. You'll take probably five steps and reach the mat around the beam."

"Five steps. Got it. What then?"

"You'll need to step up. Remember that mat will give a little, so don't fall. It's about three steps to the edge of the beam from there."

"Five steps, step up, three steps. Easy."

Mitchell sighs in response.

"What? Do you not trust your own measurements?"

"I told you I don't. I don't like this at all, Piper."

I step in his direction, letting his energy guide me to him. "I highly doubt Natalie is armed. The worst that can happen to me is I fall and hit my head." Wouldn't be the first time I got injured on the job.

"Use your senses. They've been strong. Trust them." He runs his hand up and down my arm. "They even gave you Natalie Courtwright's name when Paige didn't want to say it."

"That was pretty awesome." Of course, if you consider I can usually look at a list of names and see who's important to a case, my senses have a lot to make up for.

Mitchell doesn't say anything.

"Stop stalling. We have work to do."

"All right. I'll position myself so I'm facing you at all times. That way I'll know if you get into any trouble."

"You were tempted to say *when* I get into trouble, weren't you?"

"I thought you said no more stalling." He puts his hand on the small of my back and leads me from the room.

"Funny how you listen when it suits you."

"We're passing the uneven bars now."

I listen to the sounds of the gymnast on the bars. She's definitely new to the sport, so probably not one of the twins. I get the feeling Valentina and the twins are on the competition team, but there are other athletes who aren't at that level yet. "She's going to fall," I say.

"What?" Mitchell asks right before there's a slam on the mat.

"I'm okay," a girl yells.

"You knew she was going to fall," Mitchell says. "How?"

"I just sensed it. Her movements didn't sound fluid on the bars." That must be how Isabelle coached. It makes sense to me now. She could probably hear that something was off and tell the athlete to adjust their hand position or body weight to fix it before they fell. "Isabelle was really amazing."

THERE'S MORE THAN ONE WAY TO SENSE A KILLER

"Are you channeling her again?" Mitchell asks.

"Not really. I just understand her."

He squeezes my elbow. "We're at the balance beam now. Do you remember—"

"Five steps left, step up, three steps," I say, though I'm a little insulted he thinks I might have forgotten in a matter of a couple minutes.

"Good luck," he says. Then his voice gets louder. "Natalie Courtwright?"

"Yes." Her tone is full of both confusion and annoyance, like she can't believe he had the audacity to bother her while she's coaching.

I wait until Mitchell's voice stops moving away from me, and then I start my steps. It helps that the twins are talking beside the beam. I use their voices as guides. Not that I don't trust Mitchell's guestimate, but if you ask him he'll probably say he's six-two when, really, he's six foot.

"Hi," I say as I approach.

Both girls stop talking.

"I'm Piper. You must be Mindy and Mandy."

"Yeah, we are," one of them says. "Do you need help?" A hand reaches for me.

"Thank you. I appreciate it." While I normally don't like people touching me, I welcome the opportunity to get a better sense of this girl. She seems genuinely concerned for me. "Are you Mindy or Mandy?" I ask.

"Mindy."

"Nice to meet you. Coach Rudolph said she was working with you on the beam."

"We call her Coach Paige. We always use first names here."

"Well, not always," Mandy says.

"Right. Coach Courtwright is the exception. She thinks it's better for us to be in professional mode at all times."

"I heard she changed Valentina's routine on beam. Was Valentina struggling with the old one?"

"Not really," Mindy says. "She had a little trouble learning the dismount, but I'm sure she would have gotten it. She just needed some time to practice."

"Coach Courtwright said we couldn't chance it, though. She wants our routines to be flawless, even if it means sacrificing difficulty."

"Why is that?" I ask.

"Coach Isabelle was all about taking risks. Going for the big routines that would either make us look like superstars or cause us to flop," Mandy says.

"Sounds risky," I say.

"She believed in us. No one's ever flopped in competition," Mindy says.

Their back and forth seems to be normal for them. Kind of the equivalent of finishing each other's sentences, but in this case, it's continuing each other's conversation instead.

"Sounds like you girls miss Coach Isabelle." I step closer to the beam and reach out for it.

"Here, do you want to steady yourself on the beam?" Mindy asks me.

"Yes, please." I hate coming across as helpless, but right now it's going to allow me to have a vision without the twins knowing what I'm up to.

"To answer your question," Mandy says, "we miss Isabelle a lot. She—"

I don't hear the rest of what Mandy says because I give myself over to the vision.

"Come on, Valentina. I know you can hit this landing. You need to come out of the turn a split second sooner." Isabelle taps her open palm against the balance beam.

"I'm tired, Izzy. We've been at this for hours."

"Go home then. We'll start fresh in the morning."

"Tomorrow is Sunday."

"So? Do you want to beat Rebel or not? I'll bet you anything Tessa will be at the gym tomorrow."

"I don't care! I won't be. Let Tessa win." Valentina runs out.

"You don't mean that!" Isabelle calls after her.

"You're going to drive these girls to quit," Natalie says, coming up behind Isabelle.

"She's my sister. I know what I'm doing."

"She hates you, you know. When we lose her and the meet, it's going to be your fault."

"I've never lost on beam. Ask Phoebe and Skylar. I don't plan to lose as a coach either."

"Piper?" Mindy asks. "Are you okay?"

I sense Mitchell's presence before he reaches me.

"Sorry. I'm a little lightheaded today."

"Girls, why don't you take a break?" Natalie says. "Grab some water and stretch."

"Yes, Coach Courtwright," Mindy and Mandy say in unison.

"They're great girls," I say. "They must be easy to coach."

"They are. I'm trying to work on their technique, polish it up a bit. They lost some of that with their former coach."

"How so?" I ask, wanting to see if what Natalie says matches what the girls told me.

"She liked to go for really big routines that sacrificed the precision our athletes usually have."

"I figured Isabelle coached the girls to be a lot like how she was back in her day. Did she lack precision then?"

"She almost lost on beam to Phoebe Billings because she went for such a tough routine. Same with the floor routine against Skylar Harris. Isabelle took too many risks."

"Some might say that's why she was so good," Mitchell says. "If I recall correctly, she beat both Phoebe and Skylar every time."

"Yeah, and look at what it cost her," Natalie says.

"What do you mean by that?" I ask. Did she accidentally say more than she should have? If she and Phoebe really did conspire to kill Isabelle, this might be the slipup we need to prove it.

"She wasn't only a risk taker in the gym. She was in her personal life, too. I'll bet you anything that car accident was Isabelle's fault."

"Have you ever driven with her?" Mitchell asks.

"No, but I heard Phoebe and Skylar talking about the accident at a meet. They both thought Isabelle was to blame, too. I guess they were forced to carpool to a meet once. They said Isabelle was a terrible driver, didn't use a turn signal, and she cut people off. I believe it. The girl was reckless."

"I'm surprised competitors who didn't otherwise get along would carpool to a meet like that," Mitchell says.

"Phoebe and Skylar were traveling together. Their car broke down, and Isabelle was there when it happened. She offered to drive them."

"That was nice of her," I say.

"I guess. But what decent person wouldn't do the same?" Natalie says.

I can't help wondering if she would have left her competition stranded on the side of the road in hopes of getting a guaranteed win.

"So Phoebe and Skylar were friends then," Mitchell says.

"Yeah."

"What about Isabelle? Was she friendly to the other two girls?" Mitchell asks.

"To the casual observer, yes. But when you beat someone all the time, it's easy to smile at them, right? It doesn't make you a good person."

Wow, she really didn't like Isabelle. But if the story she told us is true, I want to talk to Chad Hooper even more than I did before. My senses drew my attention to the car accident, which means it's somehow connected to Isabelle's murder. But if the accident really was Isabelle's fault in some way, that might change everything.

CHAPTER FOURTEEN

Mitchell and I head to my office so I can get a break from everything. The problem with my senses being on high alert is that I really am getting lightheaded from all the energy coming at me. I never realized how much I was actually censoring it before, but it's clear to me now that I was doing a much better job than I thought I was at protecting myself from other people's energy.

We skipped lunch, so Mitchell orders us coffee and pastries from Marcia's Nook along with a few slices of pizza from the nearest pizza place. It's all being delivered to my office so we can just relax.

"I don't want to be a pain and ask how you're doing, but I don't want to seem insensitive either," Mitchell says.

"It's weird because I like how easily some things are coming to me, but at the same time, it's a lot to take. As soon as I stop for a moment, I realize how much is being hurled at me at every second. Isabelle is lucky she wasn't psychic."

"Maybe not. If she was psychic, she might have been able to stop the accident that caused her vision loss and maybe even her murder." Mitchell will never give up on the idea that psychics should be able to prevent their own deaths. It started with his mother, and while he's come to terms with her death the best he can, he worries about me now. I've almost died more than once since Mitchell and I met. So has he, though. Our line of work is risky. We chase after killers, which often makes us targets.

"After we eat, I want to head to Isabelle's apartment. I need to spend some time there."

"Do you think being in her space will help your eyesight return? Because I was thinking it might actually be the opposite. You might need to separate yourself from Isabelle to stop channeling her."

I sit up straight in my chair. "Don't go getting soft on me now. I have to do this. We agreed on the plan together. In order for me to fully understand what life was like for Isabelle, I need to step into her shoes completely."

"Well, Phoebe Billings hates you, so you definitely stepped into Isabelle's shoes in that regard."

"Why does competition make people act so ugly?" I ask.

"You aren't competitive?" His tone is questioning, like he's trying to prove I am competitive. "How do you explain Officer Andrews?"

Officer Andrews was a member of the WPD when Mitchell and I first started working together. He hated me. Sure, I read him against his will and found out he liked to frequent strip clubs and wasn't faithful to his wife. But to my credit, I never told his wife that. Still, we butted heads so often he requested to be transferred to Tillboro Hills. I kind of feel bad about it, mostly for the residents of Tillboro Hills, though. That includes a local author named Madison Kramer and her husband, Trevor, whom I met on a previous case when she did a book signing here in Weltunkin. Maddie and I probably would have been good friends if she lived here. We worked really well together, and she even let me know how Mitchell felt about me. She saw the spark between Mitchell and me right away. I, on the other hand, didn't realize I was in love with him until I thought he was going to die. I'm a little slow at interpreting my own feelings.

"Okay, fine. I can get competitive."

"You did at the gym today when Savannah was hitting on me." I can tell he's leaning closer to me by the sound of his voice.

"Speaking of that, as a married man, you should have stopped her." I lean back in my chair, creating distance between us again.

"I fully intended to, but I could tell you wanted to put the girl in her place. You definitely did, too."

"Believe me when I say I didn't want to be in a situation to have to put anyone in their place. You know I never liked you flirting with other women."

"I do know that. I knew it back then, too. Sometimes, I would do it to try to get you to admit you liked me. You were a tough cookie, though. You always acted disgusted with me."

"That's because I was disgusted with you," I say.

Someone knocks on the office door.

"I'll get it, and I don't believe that for a second. At least not after we became friends."

"Pizza delivery for Detective Brennan," a male voice says.

"Thank you. Keep the change."

"Wow. Thank you."

"How much did you over tip him?" I ask.

"I don't over tip. Most people just don't properly tip, so it makes me look generous in comparison." Mitchell's footsteps get closer, and then I hear a cardboard pizza box being placed on my desk. The smell is fantastic.

"They used extra garlic in the sauce."

"How can you tell? You haven't even tried it yet," Mitchell says. The lid of the box hits the desk, and the smell of garlic gets stronger.

"How can you not tell?" I ask, inhaling deeply.

Mitchell chuckles. "I've never met a woman more in love with food than you. Here. I put a slice on a plate right in front of you."

"Does it bother you that I'm not the type to eat lettuce and nothing else?"

"No, I love that you eat like a college wrestler trying to bulk up."

"Good because I have no plans of changing."

Mitchell's chair slides on the floor, which means he's sitting down again. "Mmm." His mouth is definitely full.

"Don't burn yourself. You know you're delicate. And where are the drinks?" I ask.

He slides a cup across my desk. "Left hand."

I reach with my left hand and find the drink. "Strawberry lemonade?" I ask.

"Don't tell me you smelled that, too," he says.

"Okay, I won't tell you, but I did."

"This is crazy. You're seriously superhuman."

Another knock sounds on the office door, but this time someone enters. "Delivery," Jax says.

"Hi, Jax. New cologne?" I ask.

"Yeah. You like it?"

I actually prefer when people don't wear cologne or perfume. The scent can be too much for me and give me headaches, but this one is subtle.

"I can't even smell it," Mitchell says.

"I like it. It's not overpowering."

"I have two extra-large toasted almond coffees and two pieces of—"

"Strawberry cheesecake," I say with a smile. "Bring it over."

"I guess you were waiting for these."

"She didn't even know what we were getting. Marcia said she'd surprise us," Mitchell says.

"Huh. How did you do that? Did you have a psychic vision?" Jax asks.

I shake my head. "No, my already sensitive nose is even more sensitive without my sight."

"Oh, I've heard about that. How losing one sense will heighten others to compensate. Cool."

"What's that look for then?" Mitchell asks him.

"I just remembered I didn't put any cologne on this morning. I think Piper is smelling my deodorant."

Mitchell laughs. "You smelled his armpits."

"I did not." I swat my hand in his direction and just barely manage to connect with the tip of his nose.

"Ow, nails," he says.

"You deserved it. Jax, thank you for the food. Please tell Mitchell how much he owes you and tip yourself well."

"Can't. I was told not to take any payment at all, and while you two can be scary, Marcia is scarier." His retreating footsteps tell me he's already on his way out.

"Tell Marcia I said this isn't over, and she just declared war," Mitchell says.

"I'll tell her you said thank you," Jax replies, and then I hear the door click shut.

"She's going to hide her tip jar from you," I tell Mitchell.

"I'm not afraid of her."

I laugh. "You totally are." I reach out with my hands. "Cheesecake me."

"You haven't even finished your pizza."

"So? Dessert first. You're not my father."

"Thank goodness for that." He slides a pastry box toward me and hands me a fork. The second piece is mine. Don't even think about eating it."

"Then I suggest you eat dessert first because I can't see what I'm eating. If both wind up in my belly, I really can't be held accountable."

Dad shows up at the office just as we're throwing away our garbage. "What goodies did I miss out on, and why did no one tell me to get here sooner?"

"Pizza and strawberry cheesecake. And why are you upset? You had calzone for lunch. I can smell it on your breath. Did you eat garlic knots, too?"

"It's freaky, right?" Mitchell asks. "It's like the more time that passes, the more Piper's abilities strengthen."

"That's interesting," Dad says, taking a seat at his desk. "Are you at all worried that your senses are compensating a little too well."

His true worry about the matter comes off him in waves of energy. "You think my senses are reacting this way because I'm not going to get my eyesight back."

"What?" Mitchell asks. "That can't be true. Nurse Vera said there is nothing physically wrong with Piper's eyes. This isn't permanent."

"Maybe you should talk to a therapist, pumpkin. If this is psychological, it might help to speak to a professional who can possibly figure out what's causing it."

"There is no way I'm sitting on a therapist's couch so she can ask me a ton of personal questions and tell me all the things that are wrong with me and try to prescribe tons of medications that will supposedly cure me but will actually keep me thinking there's something wrong with me so I continue to seek her help."

"That was the longest sentence in the world," Mitchell says.

"Not even close. The longest sentence in a book written in English is believed to be close to fourteen thousand words. My sentence was probably only sixty-something words."

"Why am I not surprised you know that?" Mitchell asks. "I think Dad's suggestion is a good one. You can find someone who doesn't prescribe medication. No one is going to force you to take anything."

"I have a friend, and old colleague who retired to Delaware. He mentioned a psychologist a relative of his uses. She does a lot of sessions over the phone. You wouldn't even need to go anywhere. I could get her name for you."

"No. There's nothing wrong with me. My senses are limiting my eyesight so I can focus on what I need to in order to solve this case. It's that simple."

"Okay, pumpkin. I'm going to keep making calls and

see if I can track down Chad Hooper for you. He's sort of gone off the grid, though. I can't find a single person who seems to know where he is."

"Mitchell and I are headed to Isabelle's apartment. We're staying over so I can fully immerse myself in her life and space." It gets quiet, and I know Dad and Mitchell are communicating somehow. "That's really rude, you two."

"We love you, pumpkin. You can't ask us not to worry about you."

I get up from my chair. "I can ask that you do it to my face, though." I walk to Dad's desk, and he stands up to hug me.

"You're right. I'm sorry. Be careful, though." He lets go of me.

"I will. This case will be solved by the end of the week."

"What?" Mitchell asks me.

"That sort of slipped out."

"The end of the week as in Friday?" Dad asks. "Or do you mean Saturday?"

"I don't know. My senses are just saying the end of the week. So this is going to be over soon. You guys won't have to worry about me after that."

"It's like she doesn't know us or herself," Mitchell says.

"Ha-ha. Let's go, chauffeur."

"Good luck," Dad says, and I know he means with me. I shake my head.

Mitchell helps me into the car and then slips his hand

in mine. "I know you're scared, Piper. You can put on a brave face for your dad, but you aren't fooling me. You're hoping staying at Isabelle's apartment will fix this, but you're also terrified it won't."

How can I not be? Mitchell might be impressed with my senses and how they're trying to stay tuned in to help me, but I don't think I can keep going like this. I'll burn out, and then what? What will be left of me if I wind up losing my psychic senses as well?

CHAPTER FIFTEEN

Mitchell and I get settled into Isabelle's apartment. According to Mitchell, Officer Gilbert is inside the house with Valentina. Officer Lewalski will come around nine o'clock tonight to relieve him until morning. Mr. and Mrs. DiMarco asked us to stay out here so we don't upset Valentina. She's really shaken up over my vision at the police station. I feel awful for upsetting her, but I'm also glad she's taking this seriously. She needs constant supervision, or she will end up being kidnapped. I feel strongly about that.

Since the couch is where Isabelle was murdered, we can't exactly sit there, and there's no way I'm sleeping in Isabelle's Murphy bed either, which is still put away. Mitchell and I brought an air mattress to use.

He finishes blowing it up and pats the top twice with his open palm by the sound of it. "I think that should do it.

It's sort of like a trampoline. I'm afraid you'll bounce me right off it during the night."

"Gymnastics humor while investigating the death of a former gymnast. Cute."

"You can't see me, but I'm smiling because you called me cute."

"In case you aren't looking directly at me, I'm rolling my eyes."

He laughs, and I feel his energy move toward me. "When am I not looking at you?" His hands rest on my waist. "How do you want to handle this?"

Usually, I'm the one to quickly turn to work mode when Mitchell gets all sweet and sappy, so I'm surprised he does it. Maybe he's as uncomfortable in a dead girl's space as I am. Keeping my promise not to read him, I'm doing my best not to sift through his various emotions at the moment. "I still can't believe the chief is letting us do this. We're totally contaminating a crime scene. I bet it's driving Detective O'Reilly crazy."

"Good." He lets go of my waist.

"You're going to have to get over this. I didn't think to wear a bullet-proof vest either on that case. I'm just as much to blame as she is. And she protected me with her body. She could have died."

"You're my wife. I can't stay mad at you, and I need to take my anger out on something, so I choose the careless detective who should have known better."

I reach for him, making contact with his chest. I adjust my hands to find his arms and pull him to me.

He wraps his arms around me. "I still have nightmares about it. Finding you..." He clears his throat.

"I know. Mitchell, when I had the vision of you dying, it was the most awful thing I've ever experienced. I understand." I reach for his face. "But we both have to be able to move past these incidents."

"Or we could quit our jobs and run away to a Caribbean island."

I laugh. "You do remember our honeymoon, right? Cases find us no matter where we go. This is our life. We need to accept it and learn to deal with it." I lean my head against his chest.

"All right. Let's start by dealing with this case. Do you want to read something else of Isabelle's?"

"Yeah." I lift my head, and he cups my face before kissing me.

"Okay, now I'm ready," he says. "Do you want me to find something for you to read?"

"No. I need to wander the space and reach out with my senses in hopes that something will call to me."

"Here. Loop your left arm through mine so I can make sure you don't bump into anything without interfering with your abilities." His elbow gently nudges my arm, and I take it.

"The couch is directly in front of us."

"That much I know. I can feel the energy coming off it."

"Isabelle's or the killers?"

"Both. Isabelle never woke up. She was hit and knocked unconscious. Then the killer hit her again, cracking her skull."

"Piper, how are you doing this? You aren't even touching the couch."

"I know. I can feel all the energy, and the events that played out here are just unfolding before me."

"But you can't see the killer?"

"No. I feel their rage."

Revenge.

"My senses are saying this person wanted revenge."

"Which is why Phoebe Billings is our top suspect. She's a former gymnast, so she's light on her feet, which you said the killer was. You also said the DVD Isabelle was watching set off the killer. That's when they struck."

"Yes, but there is another possibility. I'm only speculating here, but what about the truck driver? Coverage of the car accident was all over the news at the time, I'm sure. Chad Hooper lost everything because of the accident, and if he really doesn't believe he was to blame for it, then he might be angry enough to want to hurt Isabelle."

"Maybe he came here to see how she turned out after all these years. I mean, he lost his home, his job, everything, yet Isabelle was coaching and had this place. Maybe that's what set him off."

I take a step toward the couch, hoping to zero in on the rage I feel. "There's so much anger." I'm afraid to get too close to the couch. I don't want to take on the killer's anger. I'd rather focus on Isabelle. I back up.

"What is it?" Mitchell asks.

"We have to stay here together tonight, but I don't want to be overcome with the killer's rage and then..." I pause, not able to finish my statement. Isabelle was murdered in her sleep. I hate to say I don't trust myself with Mitchell once he falls asleep, but I've had killers overwhelm me before to the point where I don't know what I'm doing. I'm not willing to put him in danger.

He turns me around. "Okay, I get it. Let's find something else. What are you drawn to?"

I reach out with my right hand. "What's that way?" I ask.

"A closet. You want to check it out?"

"Yes."

He brings me to it. "Should I open the doors? They're bifold. The closet is almost the length of one wall."

I lower my hand to where I think the doorknobs would be. Mitchell moves my arm about six inches to my right. "I think whatever I need to see is inside the closet. You can open it."

The doors creak on the tracks as Mitchell slides them open. "Okay, there's a lot of gymnastics leotards. Is that the word?"

I step toward the closet. One thing in particular is

calling to me. I reach for it. The material is silky smooth. "What is this?" I ask.

"That's a leotard."

"This is what I need to read."

Someone knocks on the door.

"Hang on. Let me see who that is. Don't go having a vision while I answer the door."

I wouldn't risk that not knowing who is on the other side of the door. I hate spectators when I'm having a vision. I'm really only comfortable with Mitchell or maybe Dad around for them. "Go," I say when he doesn't move.

His footsteps sound across the floor. I bend down and run my left hand over the flooring. It feels like laminate or vinyl. I'm not sure which. But I'm assuming Isabelle wanted that because she'd be able to hear footsteps across it. Carpet absorbs sounds, but that would hinder Isabelle further since her sight was already an issue.

So how did the killer manage to remain soundless, or was the television noise enough to cover the sound of the footsteps? I turn around and try to make my way toward the coffee table. I want to check the volume on the TV.

My leg bumps into the coffee table. "Ow."

"Piper." Mitchell hurries to my side.

"Is she okay?" I recognize Officer Lewalski's voice.

"I'm good. Just feeling a little clumsy."

"You can hardly call it clumsiness when you don't know where you're going," Officer Lewalski says. "Cut yourself some slack, Piper."

"Thanks. Are you here to relieve Officer Gilbert?"

"Yeah, I thought I'd check on you guys first. See if you need anything."

"Do you happen to have two working eyeballs with you?"

"I do, but I'm currently using them myself," Officer Lewalski jokes.

I laugh.

"Hey, why do you laugh at his jokes and not mine?" Mitchell asks.

"His are actually funny," I say without hesitation.

"Well, I don't want to get in the middle of a fight between you two, so if you're good, I'm going to head to the main house. Before I go, Piper, is there anything I should know about guarding Valentina?"

He's asking if I sensed when or how she'll be abducted. "Sorry but I didn't see how it happens. She was already in the trunk of a car when I saw her in my vision."

"Okay. That's still something. I'll keep a look out for any cars that pull up outside."

"Good luck," Mitchell tells him.

"Same to you guys. You have the harder job."

I'm not so sure. I don't think keeping Valentina safe is going to be as simple as any of them believe it will be. I listen for the sound of the door closing before telling Mitchell, "I'm worried it won't be enough."

"What won't be?" His footsteps get closer.

"All of this. Guarding Valentina. Us identifying the killer."

Mitchell rubs my arm. "How can't it be enough?"

"I just have a bad feeling."

"Let's keep working. It's really all we can do right now. Why were you over here by the coffee table anyway?"

"I want to check the TV volume. I have to know if that's what stopped Isabelle from hearing her killer come into the apartment and walk around."

"Okay." Mitchell must grab the remote control because a few seconds later, the television turns on. "The DVD is still in."

"Play it," I say.

Sounds of a gymnastics meet fill the room. The volume isn't overly loud, but if the killer was being careful, and I know they were, I can see how the footsteps would be drowned out by the DVD.

"What's on the screen?" I ask.

"It looks like a compilation of both Isabelle's meets and Valentina's. Someone cut this together."

"Obviously not Isabelle, so who?" I ask.

"Maybe someone at Extreme," Mitchell says.

No.

"Try again. My senses say no."

"Could they maybe just tell us who then?" he jokes.

Paige Rudolph.

"Ask and you shall receive. It was Paige Rudolph."

"Are you serious? Your senses just answered me?"

"Yup. I guess they like you."

"Why would Paige do this? Do you think Isabelle asked her to?"

Yes.

"You're on a roll."

"They answered again?"

"Yup. What else do you want to know? Who the killer is maybe? Try that one."

"Who's the killer?"

I wait for my senses to chime in, but I don't get anything this time. "Apparently, your luck ran out."

"That's okay. I'm going to call Paige Rudolph and see if we can find out why she put this together for Isabelle." His phone beeps as he dials on speaker.

"You had her contact info on hand?"

"Yeah, your dad got everyone's numbers for us, remember?"

"I didn't know you were carrying them around."

"Hello?" Paige answers.

"Paige, this is Detective Brennan. Do you remember me?"

"Yes, of course."

"Piper and I found a DVD that seems to be a compilation of Isabelle's and Valentina's routines on the balance beam."

"Oh, yeah. Isabelle asked me to put that together for her. She wanted to compare their performances. She said she could tell something didn't sound right to her when

Valentina performed."

"Does the DVD include the performance from the night of Isabelle's car accident?" I ask.

"Yes. It includes all of Isabelle's competitions over the years. It's quite long."

That could mean Phoebe is the killer and seeing herself lose the beam to Isabelle set her off.

"Valentina's performance in the upcoming meet is an exact replica of Isabella's from the night of the car accident," Isabelle says.

Car accident.

Why can't I figure out why the accident is so important? All I know is it wasn't an accident. I need to find Chad Hooper and talk to him. No, I need to read him so I can see the accident from his perspective and get to the truth.

"Does Rebel Gymnastics have any idea that's the routine Valentina plans to do?" Mitchell asks. Clearly, his focus is still on Phoebe Billings. I get why. Losing to Isabelle was bad enough, but Tessa losing to Valentina with the same routine would be a slap in the face.

"Wait. Didn't Natalie change Valentina's routine?" I ask.

"Well, yeah. She didn't think Valentina could handle it. It is a very complicated routine. I get why Natalie is worried, but I think Valentina's new routine is too easy. I plan to talk to Natalie about it and see if we can come up with a compromise."

"Isn't the meet on Saturday?" Mitchell asks. "Valentina couldn't possibly learn a new routine by then."

"These athletes train day and night, Detective. Plus, a combination of both routines she already knows wouldn't be that complicated."

"Thank you for your time, Paige. We appreciate it," Mitchell says before ending the call.

"You were kind of abrupt with her," I say.

"I want to look into Natalie Courtwright. I feel like she's up to something. She has to have an in with someone at Rebel. Her tampering with Valentina's routine feels too much like she's trying to make sure Valentina doesn't win that event."

"You do that. Can you bring me back to that leotard first? I need to read it."

"How about you read it first? I want to keep an eye on you while you do." He takes me by the elbow and brings me back to the closet. The sound of a plastic hanger on a metal bar alerts me that he's removed the leotard from the closet. "I think you should sit down on the air mattress while you do this."

"Afraid I might try some front aerials or something?" I joke.

"That would be a sight. Just humor me, please."

"Fine." I know it's a straight shoot from the closet back to the air mattress, so I start walking.

"Stop," Mitchell says before I walk into it.

I bend down, feeling around with my hands, and then

sit on the mattress. I'm jolted upward when Mitchell sits beside me. "Wow, this thing really is bouncy like a trampoline."

"I told you." He's on my right side, and I'm sure it's intentional. He wants to be close enough to stop the vision if it gets bad. "I'm keeping my hand on your arm just in case. Don't bother arguing. You already lost your sight. I'm not taking any more chances."

I don't protest. When I hold out my right hand, Mitchell places the leotard on it, and his own hand slides down to my forearm.

Phoebe and Skylar approach Isabelle.

"I hear your routine is off the charts as far as difficulty goes," Phoebe says.

"It's challenging," Isabelle says. "Good luck to you both."

"Break a leg," Phoebe tells her. "Literally. I hope you break a leg trying to pull off the impossible. It would suit you right."

Skylar smiles and nods.

"Come on, guys. You know we don't pick our own routines. I'm just doing what they tell me to do."

"Yeah, don't act like you're not loving every second of it. Skylar worked countless hours on that floor routine by the way. The one you beat her on by a tenth of a point. She should have won."

"You were great, Skylar," Isabelle says. "I was really impressed."

Skylar lowers her head. "Not great enough."

"No one ever seems to be with Isabelle around," Phoebe says. "You enjoy trying to make us look mediocre, but one day it will come back to bite you. Mark my words. And I'll be there to see it."

CHAPTER SIXTEEN

I hand the leotard to Mitchell after the vision ends.

"What happened?" he asks. "You didn't move or anything. It was like you were in a trance."

"I was observing the whole thing. I wasn't any of the girls."

"Which girls?"

"Phoebe and Skylar approached Isabelle at the meet. Isabelle had just beaten Skylar on the floor routine. Beam was up next, and Phoebe was worried. She criticized Isabelle for going for such an intense difficulty level on the beam and said one day pushing the difficulty was going to hurt her. Phoebe said she'd be there to watch that happen."

"See. It has to be Phoebe. She's been in almost every one of your visions. She had it out for Isabelle seven years ago, and she still hated her right up until Isabelle died. It makes sense."

"In theory, yes. But we still have no proof."

"We should try to get some sleep. Tomorrow is going to be a long day." Mitchell stands up, making the air mattress lift me a bit in the process. A few seconds later, the plastic hanger clinks against the metal rod in the closet. Then the door creaks closed. "Lie down. I brought a light-weight blanket. I'll cover you."

I feel the air mattress, trying to determine which way I'm supposed to lie down. Once I'm in position, Mitchell places the blanket on top of me. Then he lies down beside me.

"I know you're not a cuddler, but being that this is an air mattress, we might be safer cuddling together. Other-wise, one of us will probably be flung off this thing."

I don't think I'll actually be able to sleep much tonight anyway, but I scoot closer to him. He wobbles backward and laughs. I grab his arm, which he wraps around me. "Better?"

"Much." He kisses my head. "Goodnight, Piper."

"Goodnight, Mitchell."

It only takes him a few minutes to fall asleep. His rhythmic breathing is soothing. I try to use it to lull myself to sleep, but I just can't. The energy in this place won't allow me to rest. Maybe this was a bad idea. Maybe I'm desperate to get my sight back, and I was willing to try anything to make that happen. So far, being in Isabelle's space hasn't helped me. I still can't see a thing unless I'm having a vision. I'm not sure how Isabelle didn't let this drive her crazy. She was able to see for years. She knew exactly what she lost in that accident. It had to be maddening.

Valentina said Isabelle changed. It was like Valentina lost her sister to that accident. I don't think Valentina knew how right she was. Isabelle changed because of it. She pushed Valentina to work harder because she herself couldn't. She tried to overcompensate for all she'd lost and live vicariously through her sister. It wasn't fair to Valentina, yet I'm not sure Isabelle realized that. I think maybe she did start to become the way Phoebe saw her all along. Hungry to win. Determined to push the limits.

At some point during the night, I do manage to fall asleep. I have to position myself with my head on Mitchell's chest to block out all the energy in the room but his. He wraps his arms around me, and all I wind up feeling is how much he loves me and how happy he really is. It's crazy to think that I'm capable of making him feel this way. Most days, I'm still not sure how he and I got to this point.

Mitchell wakes up first. He kisses my head and brushes some stray pieces of hair from my face. "How did you sleep?" he asks in his morning voice, which is slightly deeper than his regular voice.

"Better than expected." I keep my eyes closed. I know better than to think my sight will be miraculously restored, but my stomach still sinks when I finally convince my eyelids to open.

"My rock-hard pecs weren't uncomfortable?" he jokes.

I sit up quickly, and the air mattress dips next to me. Then there's a thud. "Did you just roll off the air mattress?"

"More like your movement sent me rolling off it. Next time, give a guy a warning before you make any sudden moves."

"I'm hoping there won't be a next time. I miss my bed. And Jez."

"Don't tell Jez, but I much prefer having you sleep on me. You didn't drool the way she does." Mitchell's phone rings. "It's your dad," he tells me before answering.

"I think I found where Chad Hooper has been working," Dad says. "I'm going to text you the address now."

"Great. Thank you," Mitchell says. "Piper and I are going to run home to get cleaned up, and then we'll go talk to Chad."

"Any luck last night?" Dad asks.

"Not much," I tell him.

"Good morning, pumpkin."

"I'm still blind, so it's not really a good morning."

"I'm sorry, sweetie. Try to focus on the case. Once you solve it, things should work themselves out. I'm heading to the office to take care of a job we have."

"Thanks, Dad. I appreciate you keeping up with the agency for me."

"No problem."

"How's Jez?"

"She misses you guys, but she and Max are really cute together. They shared his dog bed last night. We might need to get them married after this."

"How are we going to separate them if they get so used to being together?" Mitchell asks.

"Don't worry. Jez is like her mommy. She likes her space."

"That's true, and she loves me best," Mitchell says. "No offense to Max, but he just can't compete with me."

"This conversation is making me uncomfortable, so I'm going to hang up now. Talk to you both later," Dad says.

"Way to embarrass yourself by acting like my parents' dog is your competition," I say, getting to my feet.

"I really thought I'd embarrass myself less often around your father once we were married."

"Well, that was your first mistake. You have more opportunities to make a fool of yourself now that you're around him more."

"Great. That makes me feel so much better."

Mitchell and I go home to shower and get dressed for the day. Then we head to the address Dad gave us for Chad Hooper.

"Maybe we should have gone back to Chad's house last night," I say. "We could have cornered him there."

"I think this is better. If we approach him at work, he'll

probably want to talk to us in private. We can basically force him to tell us what we need to know because he won't want us causing trouble at his job."

"Because he'd get fired yet again," I say. "I see your point."

The car comes to a stop in what sounds like a dirt and gravel driveway.

"Where are we exactly?" Mitchell asks. "There's no sign or anything."

"It's a fish market," I say.

"How do you know? Did your senses tell you?"

I tap my nose. "Yeah, my sense of smell."

He sniffs the air. "I don't smell anything."

I open my door, and the scent of seafood rushes into the car. "How about now?"

"Okay, that I smell. Are you going to be able to handle this?"

We had to go into a butcher shop on a previous case, and the smells nearly did me in.

I raise my shirt over my nose. "Let's make this quick."

Mitchell comes around the car to get me, and then we walk into the fish market.

"We don't open for another hour," a man calls to us.

"Are you Chad Hooper?" Mitchell asks.

"What do you want with Chad?" he asks.

"That's him," I whisper to Mitchell. "He's going to lie and try to tell you Chad isn't here."

"We need to ask Mr. Hooper a few questions. I'm

Detective Brennan with the Weltunkin PD, and this is my partner, Piper Ashwell."

"Chad isn't on the schedule today. Sorry."

"That's too bad. We actually came to talk to him about some money he's owed. We've been trying to reach him, but there was no answer at his house either." I figure a guy who's so down on his luck might respond to the prospect of some quick cash.

"Chad's not the type to play the lottery, so I think you're mistaken."

"Oh, it's not from the lottery or anything like that. It's about an old lawsuit. I really can't discuss it with you, though."

"Yeah, we should go. Chad's not here," Michell says, playing along.

"Hold up." A knife clinks against a metal countertop. "You're in the right place. I just didn't want to confirm my identity until I knew who you were and why you were looking for me. What's this about the lawsuit? Did that crazy family finally listen to reason?"

"You mean the DiMarcos?" Mitchell asks.

"Yeah, them. I didn't do anything wrong."

"Can we possibly talk away from all the fish?" I ask, struggling with the smells since I can't keep my shirt over my nose while I talk to Chad.

"We can go in the back. Follow me."

Mitchell leads me.

"Hey, is there something wrong with your vision?" Chad asks.

"I got something in my eye." I figure it's best if I don't point out any similarities between me and the young girl who lost Chad all his possessions. It wouldn't make him like me or want to open up to me.

A door swings open, the whoosh of air bringing the fish smell with it. "The boss's office is in here. He won't care if we use it. He lets me crash upstairs sometimes so I can open early in the mornings."

"Is that what you did last night?" Mitchell asks.

"Yeah. I don't have much to go home to thanks to that family, so it's not a bad deal I've got going here."

"We'd like to hear your side of that accident," I say.

Mitchell pulls out a chair for me, and I sit.

"You'd be the first. I've been trying to tell my side of the story for years. No one ever wants to listen. All they care about is that girl, but I lost more than she did that day."

"We're listening," Mitchell says.

"Start from the beginning," I add. "What do you remember?"

"I was driving on the highway, going around those turns by the mountains. Hunters like that area."

Hunters.

"A stray bullet came out of the woods and hit my windshield. Naturally, I was stunned. I swerved because I thought I hit something."

"And that actually did cause you to hit something. Isabelle DiMarco's car," Mitchell says.

"Yeah, but the weird thing is, she was turning into my lane when I swerved out of it. I'm sure of it. She didn't see me or whatever. The police didn't believe me when I told them that because I was driving a giant truck. Who wouldn't see me?"

"She was listening to music. I think she was too distracted to notice you," I say.

A chair across from me creaks. "Why is it you don't even know me, yet you believe me?"

"The hunter, the police found him, right?" I ask, ignoring his question. I don't want him to know I'm psychic. I don't think he'll take that well.

"Yeah. Ruben Ballock. If you ask me, he's the one that family should have sued. He shouldn't have been shooting toward the road."

Hunter.

"Yeah, yeah, I got it."

"Okay," Chad says, thinking I'm talking to him. "You're the one who asked, though."

"Sorry. Um, did you ever speak to Ruben?"

"No. Not really at least. I was being questioned, and I could hear this guy screaming and yelling that he didn't shoot my truck. He said he wasn't even by the road. I wanted to talk to him, but the police wouldn't allow it."

I wonder if Dad remembers how all this went down at the station. He was on the police force at the time, but it wasn't his case, so it's possible he wasn't even there when this happened.

"They matched the type of bullet to Ruben's, and that was that. He was fined and served a few months in jail. But I got hit with this lawsuit for driving over the speed limit. You show me one person on this planet who doesn't drive over the speed limit."

"Not exactly something you should say to an officer of the law," Mitchell tells him.

"It's the truth, though. We all know it. My speed had nothing to do with that accident. It was the bullet. I could have died, but no one seems to care about that."

"What about your family?" I ask.

"Don't have any left."

"Well, it seems like you have a good job here now at least," I say.

"It's all right. What about that money you mentioned?"

I probably should have thought this through because there isn't any money. "Um..."

"It's not much," Mitchell says. "Only a few hundred dollars."

"I'll take anything."

"Okay, well if you could give me an address for where I should send your check—"

"Can't I take it in cash? I don't have a bank account. You need money to open one of those."

Mitchell moves beside me, and I know he's taking out

his wallet. He counts out three hundred dollars. "I suppose that works as well. Here you go."

"Thanks. And thanks for listening. I wish you were one of the cops handling the accident seven years ago. Instead, I got some jerk named Anderson or something."

I'm sure he means Officer Andrews. And I'm not surprised. Officer Andrews was famous for closing cases as quickly as possible, usually by blaming the easiest target, whether they were guilty or not. "We're very sorry," I say, standing up. I want to get far away from this fish smell.

Mitchell walks me out, and I don't take any deep breaths until we're far from the fish market. "What did you think?" he asks me.

"I believe him."

"But your senses said the accident wasn't an accident."

"I know, which is why I want to talk to Ruben Ballock. He denied shooting Chad Hooper's truck, but my senses gave me the word hunter. It's key to solving this case."

"You think Ruben lied to the police?"

"I don't know. But I do know Officer Andrews probably took the easy way out, like he usually did."

"Which means Ruben could have been hiding something. But do you really think the accident, which we know wasn't an actual accident at all, was planned?"

No.

"What?"

"I said do you think—"

"Not you. My senses. They're saying the car crash wasn't planned."

"So it's not planned, but it's not an accident?"

Yes.

"Yes, and I have no idea what that means."

"You and me both. But the car crash is definitely linked to Isabelle's death?"

Yes.

Again, my senses are communicating with Mitchell. "I think we need to solve what really happened the night Isabelle lost her eyesight. Then we'll be able to solve her murder."

Yes.

Wonderful. Two cases for the price of one.

CHAPTER SEVENTEEN

Who would have thought that I'd be cleaning up Officer Andrews's messes after he left the WPD? I guess I should have seen it coming, but until I lost my eyesight, my psychic abilities were severely limited as far as seeing the future.

The address the WPD has for Ruben Ballock is seven years old, which means there's a good chance he's not there anymore. Especially since he served almost six months in jail for breaking the hunting laws in Pennsylvania. So I have Mitchell call Dad to get him on locating a current address.

Mitchell and I stop by Marcia's Nook for pastries and coffee. Jax runs the order out to Mitchell's patrol car for us.

"I'm not supposed to take any money," Jax says.

"You tell Marcia she has to take my money, or we

won't come to her café anymore," Mitchell says. "This is crazy. It's a business."

"She told me you've overpaid her in tips for so long you could eat for free for a year," Jax explains.

"But I'm not going to. I'll wind up paying more at a place with food and coffee that's not nearly as good, so she needs to let me pay for everyone's sake."

"Jax, tell Marcia I insisted," I say.

"This better not get me fired," Jax says.

I hear the exchange of money through the window, and then Mitchell places a bag and drink caddy on my lap.

"She won't fire you," I assure Jax.

Since we haven't heard from Dad yet, we bring the items to my office. Dad is at his computer typing away.

"Was your keyboard always this loud?" I ask.

"It's not loud. You're just overly sensitive," Dad says. "Coffee for me?"

"Um, sure," Mitchell says, and I know he just gave up his own coffee. We really should have thought to bring some for Dad.

"Okay, so finding Ruben Ballock is going to be tricky. After getting out of prison, he took up camping."

"Like as in he sleeps in a tent outside?" I ask.

"Yes. He never established a permanent residence again. Only a PO box in town."

"Are you telling us we're going to have to wander the woods to find him?" Mitchell asks.

"Or camp out at the post office until he checks his mail," Dad says. "Your choice."

"We don't have time for that. We need to know where he's camped out."

Delaware River.

"Well, okay. But where?"

"Huh?"

"Let her go. Her senses have been feeding us information pretty much for days. It's amazing," Mitchell says.

"The Delaware River is big. I'm going to need some more info," I tell my senses.

Bridge.

"By a bridge."

"At least it's not the Weltunkin Bridge," Mitchell says.

I have a lot of bad memories involving that particular bridge, which is why I avoid it at all costs.

"While this is indeed impressive, pumpkin, it's still not enough to go on."

"I'm doing the best I can," I say.

Mitchell rubs my back. "You're doing great. I'll call Wallace and get Harry on board."

"That will only help if you have something that belongs to Ruben Ballock. There's nothing for Harry to smell to pick up on Ruben's scent."

"She's right, Mitchell. I don't think Harry will be much help in this instance."

"Then how do we find him?" Mitchell's frustration hits me in a rush of energy.

I step away from him.

"Sorry," he says. "I'll get it under control." His intake of air changes, and I know he's doing deep breathing exercises to calm himself.

"Dad, what about Ruben's social media presence? Maybe he posted pictures of where he is or places he likes to hike along the Delaware River."

Hunter.

"Yeah, I get it. He's a hunter. You can stop telling me now!"

"Hold on. Maybe that's not what your senses mean," Dad says. His keyboard is clicking like crazy again.

"What are you thinking?" I ask him.

"Well, I remember there's a place along the river. It's a stop for hunters. You can't hunt in that location because it's too highly populated. Here. I got it. It's called Hunter's Heaven."

Yes.

"That's where we'll find him," I say.

"Let's go." Mitchell grabs my arm. "Dad, can you text me the address?"

"Already on it," Dad says, and Mitchell's phone dings a moment later.

"Thanks, Dad," I say.

Mitchell and I hurry back to the car. Mitchell enters the address into his navigation, and we're on the road in minutes.

I drink half my coffee and hold it out to Mitchell. "Here. I know you gave my dad yours."

"Thanks." He takes it.

I reach into the pastry bag and pull out a donut. I laugh. "Jelly donuts."

"Isabelle's favorite. When do you think your cravings will go away?"

"No idea. Maybe when my eyesight returns. Maybe neither will ever happen."

"Don't say that." His cup slides into the cup holder in the middle console. "Everything is going to work out. I'm sure of it. Now, hand me a jelly donut before you stress eat them all."

Mitchell parks outside Hunter's Heaven. "It looks like a log cabin on the outside."

"I guess that's appropriate," I say as we stand in front of the building. I don't sense many people around, but I doubt a place like this, out in the middle of nowhere, gets anyone but hunters.

"There are five steps up," Mitchell says.

I follow his lead up the steps and to the door, which he opens for us.

"Oh boy. I'm glad you can't see this."

"Deer heads on every wall?" I ask.

"Yeah, not just deer, though. And it looks like they sell everything from clothing to knives, to guns and ammo."

"No bows and arrows?" I ask.

"Oh, those two. It's basically any hunting gear you can think of, including tents."

"How would Ruben Ballock be able to afford anything in here if he lives off the land?" I ask.

"Maybe he barters for it. You know, he catches a deer and exchanges the meat for hunting gear."

"This place would lose a lot of money that way. I mean whoever owns this is probably a hunter themselves. They could catch their own meat."

"Good point. Let's find out. Your senses told us we'd find Ruben here."

"That's true."

Mitchell brings us to the register, which is currently ringing up a sale judging by the sounds it's making.

"Enjoy your hunting trip with your daughter this weekend," a man says.

"Hopefully, we'll be celebrating a win," another man responds.

"Good morning," Mitchell says. "I'm Detective Brennan, and this is Piper Ashwell. We're looking for a hunter named Ruben Ballock. Do you happen to know him?"

"Most people don't tell me their names when they come in. Unless they're buying weapons, of course. Everything here is on the up-and-up, Detective. I can assure you of that."

"That's good to hear, but maybe you know him as the guy who camps out in these woods. Ruben doesn't have a permanent residence."

"Oh, that guy. Yeah, I know who you mean, but he doesn't come in here much."

"No?"

"Nah, if you saw him, you'd understand. From what I'm told by customers, he washes his clothing in the river. He's got a campsite not far from here. Catches all his food. He doesn't really have money to shop here, though."

That makes sense. "Do you know where his camp is?" I ask.

"About two miles up the river. I don't think you can miss it. People run into him all the time."

"Thank you," Mitchell says. "We appreciate your help." We walk back outside. "I guess your senses led us here because that guy knew where to find Ruben."

"I guess."

"I hate to say this, but maybe you should wait in the car. We can't drive to this campsite, and I don't think you should be hiking."

"I have to go with you. We need my senses. This guy is a hunter. If he has any plans to turn his gun on us, I need to know before it happens."

"You suddenly have a lot more faith in your ability to see the future," Mitchell says.

"No, it's not that. I can read his emotions and know if we're in danger."

I hear laughter near the river. "What's that?"

"Teenagers." Mitchell pauses. "And they just gave me

an idea." He steps in front of me so his back is to my chest. "Hop on. I'm going to piggyback you there."

"You can't carry me that far."

"Thanks for the vote of confidence where my strength is concerned, but need I remind you that I worked out practically nonstop for the duration of my two-week suspension, and I was in pretty good shape before that?"

"Any excuse to compliment your physique," I say.

"On top of that, you barely weigh anything."

"Did you just insult me?"

"No. Only you would think a comment about you not being overweight was an insult. Just hop on. Let me show you what a strong man you married."

"I'm rolling my eyes, just so you know."

"I could have guessed. Now come on. We're wasting time."

I can't believe I listen. I loop my arms around his neck and jump up. He reaches back and grabs my legs.

"There. Easy."

"I feel ridiculous."

"It's better than looking ridiculous because you keep falling over tree roots and rocks," he says.

It takes Mitchell about thirty minutes to find Ruben's campsite. He must be ready to drop, but he never once complains. He sets me down on the ground. "We're here. I think."

More like he hopes. "Do you see him?"

"Only his tent and fire. He has water boiling in a pot at the moment."

"Boy I hope this is nothing like that show you watch where the people are out in the wilderness naked."

Mitchell laughs. "I knew you peeked during that show."

"Please, everything is blurred out anyway."

Mitchell smirks and then calls out, "Hello? Ruben Ballock?"

"Who's there?" comes a male voice. I feel the guy's energy getting closer and closer to us. He must be one of those people who doesn't understand personal boundaries.

"Are you Ruben Ballock?" Mitchell asks. He reaches out to push me slightly behind him, which means this guy has a weapon on him. I expected as much since he's a hunter.

"Yeah. Who are you?"

"Detective Brennan with the WPD. My partner and I would like to speak to you about the car crash seven years ago. We know you were charged with hunting too close to the road and firing into traffic."

"Bogus charge. I didn't shoot into traffic."

"Can you tell us what did happen, then?" Mitchell asks.

"I was hunting, but there was this other group. A man and a younger girl. The girl didn't seem very into it, but whatever. I didn't pay them much attention. When I came across them, I turned and went back in the direction I came from. You don't steal another man's hunting grounds, you know."

"So they'd already set up camp there?" I ask.

"No, they looked like they were passing through, but I didn't want to be trailing them and going after their left-overs. So I changed directions. A little while after that, I circled back around to see if they'd left. I heard the shot, so I stopped. I figured they were still there, and they got something. I went back later on, hoping to have similar luck, but the cops were all over the area. They told me I was the only hunter around. I tried to tell them someone else was there, but they said there was no sign of anyone, and since the bullet they found matched the kind I was using, they pinned the car crash on me."

"Did you have a lawyer?" I ask. It can't be Brian Clark. That much I know. I'm still convinced Clark was paid to get Chad Hooper to agree to a bad deal.

"I had to have a public defender assigned to me. I don't even remember his name, but he didn't do anything for me."

I can't figure out why my senses wanted me to come out here and see Ruben. It doesn't seem like he's lying or that he had anything to do with the car crash. It doesn't make sense. I step forward and extend my hand to Ruben. "Thank you for speaking to us."

His hand wraps around mine.

"Where were these people when I needed them seven years ago? They actually listened to me. I could have

used their help instead of that incompetent police officer's."

I let go of Ruben's hand, pretty sure I just heard his thoughts in this moment. Mitchell slips his hand around my back to guide me away from the campsite.

"What did you see?"

"Nothing. I heard his thoughts. He's telling the truth. He had nothing to do with the car crash."

Mitchell's phone rings. "Brennan." He pauses. "What? When? How did this happen?" Another pause. "We're on our way."

"What is it?" I ask.

"Valentina is missing."

CHAPTER EIGHTEEN

It takes us forty-five minutes to get to Extreme Gymnastics. Mitchell did his best to run to the patrol car with me on his back, and then he drove the rest of the way with the siren on. According to Officer Gilbert, who was watching Valentina, she was taken at the gym today when she went to use the bathroom in the locker room.

My senses told me she needed a woman to guard her, but I didn't listen to them. "I should have pushed for having Detective O'Reilly stay with Valentina. I knew this would happen. It's my fault for not insisting."

"It's not your fault Detective O'Reilly is on desk duty, and you know you can't tell Chief Johansen what to do," Mitchell says as we walk into the gym. "There's no point in blaming yourself. We need to focus all our energy on finding Valentina."

The tranquility I felt in this gym the last time we were here is gone, replaced with worry and fear.

"Brennan," Officer Wallace calls.

They must have brought in more man power to help us search the place for clues as to who took Valentina and where. Mitchell brings me over to him. "Wallace, Dad, fill us in."

"Dad is here?" I ask.

"Yes, pumpkin, I'm here. I called the station when I couldn't get through to Mitchell. Cell service must have been spotty where you were."

"Yeah, it took me a few tries to get through to you guys as well," Officer Wallace says.

"Well, we're here, so get us up to speed," Mitchell says. "Where is Gilbert?"

"I'm right here," he says from off to our left. "I was checking the locker room. I'm really sorry about this. I couldn't go into the locker room with her, though."

"That's not your fault," I say. It's mine for knowing this was going to happen. Despite what Mitchell said, I should have insisted on Detective O'Reilly being here, if only for instances like taking Valentina to the restroom.

"Valentina was working with Coach Courtwright," Officer Gilbert says. "They were on the balance beam. Valentina wasn't happy with the routine. She asked to go back to her sister's, but Natalie didn't like that idea at all."

"It's too difficult for her." I recognize Natalie's voice and turn toward the sound.

"Is it? Or are you trying to make sure Valentina can't beat Tessa on Saturday?" I ask. I'm done playing nice with these people. Valentina's life is on the line, and I need answers now.

"What exactly are you accusing me of?"

"I think you know exactly what I'm talking about. You're working with someone at Rebel Gymnastics."

"No, I'm not. They're our competition. I'd never work with them."

"Why did you insist Valentina do such an easy routine then?" It's Paige Rudolph talking now.

"Stay out of it, Paige. You have no idea what you're talking about."

"Yes, I do. What she said makes sense. Are you working with someone from Rebel? Are you trying to make sure Valentina doesn't win on beam?"

She scoffs. "That's absurd."

Lie.

"You're lying," I say.

"No, I'm not, and you can't prove it."

"I need to see the locker room," I say.

Natalie laughs. "Good luck. You can't *see* anything."

Mitchell takes me by the arm and leads me to the locker room. "No one moves," he calls over his shoulder to the others.

"I really want to smack her," I say.

"Get in line. Look, Piper, I believe you when you say Natalie is lying. I think someone is definitely working with her to sabotage Valentina, but Natalie isn't the kidnapper. Someone else took Valentina."

He's right, of course. "It has to be whomever she's working with," I say.

"But why? If they were sabotaging the routine—"

"They were trying to, but Valentina refused to go along with the easier routine, and that ruined everything."

"But she just argued with Natalie about it. How would Natalie's accomplice be able to get over here so quickly and kidnap Valentina?"

"Maybe she was already here," I say.

Yes.

"That's it. Mitchell, she was already here."

"Then it's not Phoebe Billings," he says, sounding completely shocked.

"No, I don't think it is." She's still in police custody, so she couldn't have done this.

"It has to be someone else who works here then, doesn't it?" He pushes open a door, making the hinges squeak.

"They didn't come in or out this way. That door would have gotten Officer Gilbert's attention," I say.

"There must be another exit in the back," he says, leading me through the locker room. "Stop me if you pick up on any energy you want to check out."

I reach out with my senses, but I don't get anything. Mitchell opens another door, and I feel the sunlight hit my face. Something else hits me, too. "She came out this way." I reach for the door and press my hand against it.

"Where are you? Tessa?" Valentina calls. "Tessa, I know it's you. I saw your backpack. Your name is on it."

A pillowcase lowers over her head.

I immediately let go of the door, sensing something bad was about to happen to Valentina. Like she was going to be knocked unconscious.

"Are you all right?" Mitchell asks.

"Better than all right. I just brought myself out of the vision before I was potentially knocked unconscious."

"How? Did you sense it was going to happen before it did?"

"Yeah. Like a vision inside of a vision." This is crazy. My senses have never worked this way before. "Valentina thought Tessa was here. She followed her out. But it wasn't Tessa. Someone stole Tessa's backpack to use it to lure Valentina outside where they put a pillowcase over her head and knocked her out." Which means she's probably in the trunk of that car already.

Mitchell doesn't ask who it was because it's clear I didn't see or sense the kidnapper. "I'm going to call Rebel Gymnastics and confirm that Tessa's backpack is missing."

I nod. He needs evidence. This isn't much, but at least it's something. He gets on his phone.

"You guys okay in here?" Dad calls.

I fill him in while Mitchell is on the phone. "We need

to find out who Natalie is working with from Rebel Gymnastics," I say.

Accident.

"No, no more with the accident," I say.

"Pumpkin, follow your senses. Don't argue with them."

"But we've already established the accident wasn't really an accident."

"Hey." Mitchell walks over to me and takes my hand in his. "Piper, breathe. Dad's right. You need to listen to what your senses are telling you. We'll figure it out together. Now that Valentina's been kidnapped, try focusing on what she's told you about the accident. Maybe that will help."

It's worth a shot. "Valentina mentioned she was always telling Isabelle the accident wasn't her fault."

"Right. But your senses said that wasn't true. Doesn't that mean your senses were telling you she didn't really have that conversation with her sister? She might have been lying to protect someone. Like Tessa."

"Or it could mean the accident was Valentina's fault in some way," Dad suggests.

My senses don't confirm or deny either option.

"Did you confirm that Tessa's backpack is missing?"

"No. Tessa left practice early. Her sister picked her up over an hour ago."

"Then Tessa is a suspect. It's possible Valentina did

see her. Tessa could have faked the friendship with Valentina and then tried to sabotage her routine."

"I think we need to revisit Isabelle's accident," Dad says. "Piper, you saw it. What can you tell us about it?"

"Isabelle never even heard the squeal of the truck's brakes or anything. Her music was too loud. According to the truck driver, Isabelle was coming into his lane. She didn't signal, though, so maybe she was drifting into the other lane and didn't even realize it." I don't see how this is connected. We need answers, and we need them now. "Let's play the game. Maybe we'll get something."

Mitchell rubs my back, trying to calm me since I'm clearly upset. The energy in this place is getting to me. Natalie's energy in particular at the moment. I take several deep breaths and nod to let Mitchell know I'm ready.

"What's Jezebel's favorite toy?" he begins.

"Her squeaky hamster."

"What's my brother's name?"

"Nick."

"Who is our landlord?"

"Theodore Hall."

"Was Isabelle's killer present at her car accident?"

"Yes."

"Have we met the killer yet?"

"Yes."

"Is it the hunter who shot the truck driver's windshield and caused the accident?"

"Sort of."

"What does that mean?"

Mitchell's question snaps me out of my meditative state. "I don't know."

"It could mean this person is connected to the hunter," Dad suggests. "Or that the person isn't really a hunter but was there with one."

Yes. Even though I'm not playing the game anymore, my senses clearly have more to say.

"When did we meet the killer?" I ask my senses, but Dad answers.

"Maybe at one of the gyms."

"No, not you, Dad. My senses. When did we run into the killer?"

Hunter.

"Fine, then when did we run into the hunter?"

Hunter's Heaven.

"At Hunter's Heaven. We only talked to the guy at the register."

"Then it has to be him," Mitchell says. "Let's go."

"No. That can't be right. That guy barely knew Ruben Ballock. If he's the hunter that shot Chad Hooper's windshield, he would have known all about the car crash and who was blamed for the shooting. But he didn't."

"He could have been lying."

"He wasn't. I would have known."

"Okay, but that doesn't necessarily clear him."

"Who else was there? Mitchell, you have to remember because I couldn't see anyone. Think. Try to visualize the place in your head."

"I don't have to. It was only us, the guy working the register, and that customer before us."

Yes.

"It's one of them. The hunter is one of them," I say.

"But wait. The hunter and the shooter are two different people?" Mitchell asks my senses.

Yes.

"Yes, they're connected."

"So you were right earlier. Someone helped the killer."

No.

I shake my head. "I don't understand. There are two people involved, aren't there?" I ask my senses.

No.

"Is the hunter important at all?"

Indirectly.

This is infuriating. "Why can't you just tell me? Or show me what happened?"

Mitchell wraps his arms around me. "Piper, please. You have to calm down." His grip on me tightens. He's not going to let me go until I get control of myself. "Deep breaths. Do it with me."

"You're suffocating me."

He lowers his arms instead of releasing me. I tilt my head up toward his even though I can't see his face. Right now, I really wish I could. The color green of his eyes is the most calming color in the world to me.

"You're doing great, pumpkin," Dad says, and I realize my breathing is normal again.

"How can the killer and the hunter know each other?" I ask them.

"Have you come across any hunters on this case, other than Ruben Ballock?" Dad asks.

"No," Mitchell says.

"Yes," I blurt out. "How did we forget?"

"Forget what?" Mitchell asks.

"When we were talking to Skylar Harris, her father called. She said he was on a hunting trip."

"Mr. Harris is the hunter?" Mitchell asks.

My senses start tingling like crazy. "Yes. It's him. He was also the hunter we encountered at Hunter's Heaven."

"And Tessa is his daughter, so it makes sense that he'd want her to win," Mitchell says. "He kidnapped Valentina so Tessa would win the meet on Saturday."

"He also had the money to pay Natalie to sabotage Valentina's routine on the balance beam," I add.

"And Isabelle was not only Valentina's coach," Dad says, "but she was also Skylar's biggest competition seven years ago."

"Mitchell, do you remember when I guessed exactly what the Harris household looked like?"

"Yeah, it was uncanny."

"What if I was right about them having a fireplace or

fire pit in the backyard? Mr. Harris could have burned whatever it was he used to wipe his fingerprints off that trophy, just like Detective O'Reilly suggested."

"Then we found our killer," Mitchell says.

"It's Mr. Harris," I say.

CHAPTER NINETEEN

Mitchell, Dad, and I walk out of the locker room together, ready to confront Natalie. If we can get her to admit to being paid off by Mr. Harris, we'll have proof of motive and scheming. We can get him on kidnapping charges and find Valentina. After that, we just need to prove he killed Isabelle.

"Can we go home now?" Natalie's voice carries throughout the gym.

"I'm afraid you won't be going home anytime soon," Mitchell tells her.

"Why? You have no reason to detain me. I obviously didn't do anything to Valentina. I've been here the entire time with witnesses."

"I'm sure you planned it that way. Was it one of your conditions when Mr. Harris came to you with this plan to sabotage Valentina at the next meet?"

"Mr. Harris?" Natalie's voice is full of confusion, and what's worse is it's genuine.

"Mitchell, we're wrong," I say.

"That's impossible. Piper, all the pieces fit together. Don't you remember what Mr. Harris told the guy at Hunter's Heaven? He said he and his daughter would be celebrating a victory on Sunday. He meant because Tessa is going to win the meet on Saturday."

"Then it's Tessa and Mr. Harris doing all of this?" Dad asks.

No.

"Sorry, but no. Tessa is innocent."

"Then..." Mitchell's grip on me tightens.

"It's Skylar," we both say.

Natalie gives a nervous laugh. Bingo!

"Skylar Harris is the one who's paying you," I say. "That makes sense. You guys are the same age."

"So, our age doesn't prove anything."

"I bet your bank account will prove we're right. If we check it out, we'll find some recent deposits. I'm guessing Skylar was smart enough to pay you in cash so there was no paper trail to lead back to her."

"That's a guilty look if I've ever seen one," Dad says. "Piper, you can't see it, but Natalie looks like you when Mitchell found your secret stash of dark chocolate in your desk drawer."

I like to have dark chocolate on hand to help ward off headaches caused by my visions. Oddly enough, I haven't gotten a headache on this case. My abilities are seriously amazing. It's almost like they're looking out for me because I can't see.

"You have no proof of anything," Natalie says. "All you have is the assumptions of a woman who can't see her nose in front of her face."

"Seeing your nose isn't easy to do. At least not seeing it well," Mitchell whispers to me. I know he's trying to annoy Natalie with his commentary, so I play along.

"Oh, no. Are you going cross-eyed right now? Tell me I'm not missing this because I can't see."

"He is," Dad says with a laugh.

"What is wrong with you people?" Natalie asks. "You're all seriously unhinged."

"No, what's seriously unhinged is you taking money to sabotage the girls you're supposed to be training to win. What do you think Mr. Shaw will have to say about this?"

"About what?" Mr. Shaw's voice is loud and approaching.

"Just one of your coaches here trying to make sure Extreme loses at least on beam this Saturday. Why don't you tell him, Natalie? Tell him how Skylar Harris has been paying you to mess with Valentina's routine."

"Natalie, is this true?"

"I believe it," Paige says. "Mr. Shaw, I told you the routine change Natalie made didn't make sense. I knew she was playing it too safe. Valentina is too talented a gymnast for a routine that would earn her minimal points."

"Natalie, I want an explanation," Mr. Shaw says.

"Fine. I'll tell you what happened. After Isabelle died, Valentina cracked. She couldn't take the pressure, and doing her sister's old routine was too much for her."

I have to hand it to Natalie. That would sound completely legitimate if I didn't know she was lying.

"Then why did Valentina fight with you about it?" Paige asks. "You wouldn't listen to her at all."

"Because, like I said, she was torn up over Isabelle's death, and she couldn't think clearly. Mr. Shaw, she would've gotten herself hurt if I let her do that routine. It's better to have her take a lesser score in one meet and build her confidence back up after that."

"Detectives, Natalie has been with me for a while now. I believe she was acting in the best interest of both Valentina and this gym." Mr. Shaw's tone is clear. He's going to stand by Natalie.

"So there you have it," Natalie says. "Are we finished here now? I really think you should be out there finding Valentina, not questioning me for caring about my athletes."

She's good. Completely manipulative. I reach my hand out to shake hers. "I apologize for jumping to conclusions. No hard feelings?"

"Go ahead, Natalie. Shake her hand so we can move past this," Mr. Shaw says.

Natalie huffs but takes my hand. I wrap my fingers around hers.

"Leave the money in my gym bag in the locker room. The back door is unlocked for you," Natalie says into her phone. *"I have to go. Paige is coming, and she's already suspicious."*

"You're the one who left the door to the locker room open," I say.

"That's absurd. I thought we were finished with this."

"I saw you. You were on the phone with Skylar." Okay, I'm guessing the identity of the person on the other end of the line. "You told her you left that door open so she could put the money in your gym bag."

"I knew it," Paige says. "You sold us out. These girls have trained for years, and you sold them out. How much are they worth to you? I say we check her gym bag and find out."

"I agree," Mitchell says. "Natalie, you need to escort us to your gym bag."

"No way. Where's your warrant?"

"Natalie, if you want to stay employed here, I suggest you do as they say," Mr. Shaw says. There's a subtle shift in his energy. He's questioning her after my little stunt. "If you don't have this money, your name will be cleared, and I'm sure the detectives will let the matter drop."

I'm not about to agree to that, and I'm sure Mitchell isn't either. We remain silent.

"What's the holdup?" I ask. "If you're innocent, like

216

you're insisting you are, there shouldn't be a problem. You should be happy to throw that in our faces."

"Fine. Follow me."

Mitchell walks with me. "What if it's not there? What if kidnapping Valentina was a way to avoid having to pay Natalie?" he asks.

He's right. Why would Skylar pay her if she kidnapped Valentina? We aren't going to find the money. But Natalie clearly doesn't know that. Kidnapping Valentina must not have been the plan. Skylar cut Natalie out of the deal entirely. Our only shot is to get Natalie to cooperate with us and throw Skylar under the bus.

"Natalie," I say, "wait. You might want to consider telling us what you know. I have a feeling Skylar screwed you over."

"I don't know what you're talking about," she says. The locker room door opens. "My bag is over here." Nervous energy rolls off her. She unzips the bag so slowly it barely makes a sound. Then I feel her relief when she doesn't see the money.

"I was right," I say. "Skylar decided to cut you out of the deal. She took matters into her own hands and kidnapped Valentina so she wouldn't have to pay you. How much did you lose out on?"

"I think you got her," Mitchell whispers beside me. "She's looking pretty darn angry right now, and I don't think it's directed at you this time."

That's a first.

"The Harris family is very wealthy, so I'm guessing it was a lot. You were dedicated to Extreme and its gymnasts. It couldn't have been easy for Skylar to sway you to go along with her plan."

"Natalie, I want to warn you that what Skylar did is going to cost her time in prison," Mitchell says. "You don't want to go down as an accomplice to Valentina's kidnapping."

"He's right. You have a chance to cooperate with us now. Tell us what Skylar's done. You took a bribe. You didn't kidnap anyone. Don't let Skylar's actions be your downfall."

"I didn't have anything to do with Valentina disappearing," Natalie insists.

"Prove it," I say. "Because right now, Detective Brennan doesn't believe you. Do you really want to get hauled down to the police station and questioned when you can just tell us what you do know? Make this easier on yourself. Skylar certainly isn't looking out for you. She didn't even trust you to follow through with sabotaging Valentina's routine. That's why the money isn't where you told her to put it."

"You can't possibly know—" She stops abruptly.

"I can, though. I had a psychic vision of you on the phone with Skylar. You may not believe in psychics, but the WPD believes in me. My word is going to mean a lot more to them than yours."

"She's telling the truth," Mitchell says. "So I'm going

THERE'S MORE THAN ONE WAY TO SENSE A KILLER

to offer you this chance one more time. If you don't take me up on it, I'm bringing you to the station for questioning. Since there's a young girl missing, you might want to consider getting yourself a lawyer."

"You'll need to use your own money, though, since Skylar stiffed you," I say, hoping that comment is the final nail in the coffin.

"I didn't have a choice. I'm behind on my rent. I needed money fast so I wouldn't have to move out of my apartment."

I get the sense that Natalie lives well above her means, trying to fit in with people like Skylar who have a lot more money than she does.

"How could you sell us out like that? Is that the real reason you wanted Isabelle's job as head coach?" Paige yells. For a quiet person, she's really letting loose now. "Were you scheming with Skylar all along?"

"No. I swear. She came to me one day after practice. She said she knew about my money problems. I don't know how for sure, but I'm guessing she heard me on the phone at the last meet. My landlord called me, demanding the rent I owe. She said she could help me out if I did a favor for her in return."

"So you convinced Valentina to change the routine," Paige said. "For how much?"

"Does it matter? I didn't get anything, and there's still time to fix this." Her energy shifts to desperation. "Mr.

Shaw, I can fix this. I'll work with Valentina to get her where she needs to be by Saturday."

"You can't," Paige says. "She's gone, remember?"

Gone because Natalie failed. Valentina wasn't going to go along with Natalie's new routine, and because of that, she was kidnapped. Skylar must have been here to drop off the money and changed her mind, but if that's what happened, why did she have a pillow case with her?

"Natalie, you're fired. Please clear out your locker," Mr. Shaw says.

"Mr. Shaw, please. You can't do this. I'll lose my apartment."

"You should have thought about that before you decided to betray us. You'll need to sign a nondisclosure agreement. I can't trust you not to run to Rebel and tell them all our routines without one. At least this way I'll have some legal ground to stand on if and when you try to betray us again."

Mitchell grabs my arm and leads me out of the locker room. "How do we find Skylar and Valentina now? It's clear Natalie doesn't know where they are."

I need to read something of Valentina's. "Valentina should have a locker here, right? Something of hers must be inside it. If I read it, I might be able to locate her."

"I can take you to Valentina's locker," Paige says from behind me. "Come on."

Mitchell helps me back to the locker room.

"I have a master key," Paige says, and I hear the

locking mechanism unclick as she opens the door. "She has a towel, one of those step counters, and a change of clothing. Wait. There's also this."

"What is it?" I ask Mitchell.

"A necklace. It's a gymnast charm."

"That's what I want to read," I say, holding out my hand.

A few seconds later, I feel the cold chain and charm fall onto my palm. Valentina's energy is all over it.

Darkness. The car comes to a stop. A door slams shut, shaking the car slightly.

"Let me out!" Valentina cries out.

Footsteps sound on concrete.

"Where do you want me to dump the car?"

"Not my problem. I don't want to know what you do with it. Just get rid of it. That's what I'm paying you for," Skylar practically yells.

The vision ends.

"I know what happened to the money Skylar promised Natalie. She paid someone to get rid of the car she used to transport Valentina. She told the guy to get rid of it."

"Where were they?" Mitchell asks.

"I don't know. I couldn't tell. Valentina is in the trunk, so she couldn't see anything. She only heard them talking."

"Do you know who Skylar was talking to, pumpkin?" Dad asks. I didn't even know he followed us back into the locker room. He must have returned while I was having the vision.

I try to focus on the male voice from the vision. It did sound vaguely familiar. I know I've heard it before, but it was muffled by the trunk.

"Was it Skylar's father?" Mitchell asks. "It would make sense that they were in on this together."

"No, I don't think Skylar would talk to her father that way. She viewed this guy as beneath her."

"She views a lot of people as beneath her," Paige says. "She comes across as quiet, but if you know Skylar, you know she doesn't talk to anyone she doesn't deem worthy of the effort. That's most people. She's never even said two words to me."

So unlike Phoebe, who likes to make it clear she hates someone, Skylar is the silent type who lets her emotions stew until they lash out at you. That explains my vision of Isabelle's death. Skylar was so calm. Focused. But then she just snapped and killed Isabelle in the most brutal manor, beating her skull in.

"Piper, you're breathing really heavily," Mitchell says.

I hand him the necklace. "I think I was channeling Skylar. She tries to control her emotions so much that when she loses control, it's like an explosion of rage." All the pieces of this case fall into place in my head. "I know how it's all connected. I just figured it out."

"Are you going to tell us?" Mitchell asks me.

"I will, but there's still one more thing I need to figure

out. The man she gave the car to. I know him. I've heard his voice."

Accident.

"He's connected to the car accident."

Hunter.

My mouth hangs open.

"You know who it is," Mitchell says.

"It's Ruben Ballock. He has Valentina."

CHAPTER TWENTY

Mitchell gets on his phone and starts barking orders into it.

Future.

"No. Mitchell wait. My senses are telling me my vision hasn't happened yet. It's of the future. I think Skylar still has Valentina. We need to find Skylar."

"Wallace, track Skylar Harris's car. We need to find her and make sure she doesn't leave town. If anyone spots it, you call me immediately. We think Skylar kidnapped Valentina DiMarco and is transporting her somewhere in the trunk of her car." As soon as he gets off the phone, he rubs my arm. I swear it's become his new way of communicating with me since I can't see. "We're going to find her."

I can't stand around and do nothing. "We should have someone go to Ruben Ballock's campsite as well. See if he's still there or not. I have no idea how far into the future

I saw." It's usually not far at all, so there's a good chance he's already left his campsite. Still, we have to try everything.

"I'm going to call her parents and see when they last saw her."

"Tessa," I say. "She drove Tessa home from practice."

"You think she slipped up and said something to her?"

"I don't know, but we need to find out."

"Okay, let's go."

"I'm going with you," Dad says. "I'll follow."

Mitchell throws on the siren and speeds to Tessa Harris's house. Normally, he'd be worried about Dad commenting on his driving when I'm in the car, but since we don't know how much of a lead Skylar has on us, we don't have time to obey traffic laws. We need to get to Tessa and find out what she knows, if anything. I have a bad feeling that if we don't find Valentina before my vision comes true, we won't make it to her in time. Ruben Ballock probably has no idea that he's helping the person who actually got him thrown in prison. While Mitchell drives, I fill him in on what I now know. "I'm convinced Skylar and her father were the hunters Ruben saw the day of the car crash. I think Skylar spotted Isabelle's car and tried to shoot at her rival. Only she missed and hit Chad Hooper's truck instead."

"That means Skylar hired the man she put in prison to help her dispose of Valentina's body," Mitchell says.

"And he has no idea."

"Didn't he hear Valentina in the trunk?" Mitchell asks.

"I don't think so. I think Ruben is hard of hearing." I remember how he seemed to keep walking toward us when we went to talk to him at his campsite. "I think he got so close to us because he was trying to hear what we were saying. And in my vision of Skylar and Ruben, Skylar was practically yelling. She was making sure he could hear her."

"She's framing him again. If he gets caught, it would look like he's taking revenge on the family that sent him to prison."

"Right, but really that family is the Harris family. This is all Skylar's fault."

"And he's helping her because he doesn't have a clue."

"No. He has nothing. No job. No money. So, of course, he'd take money to dump an old car."

"Old car? Skylar drives a BMW," Mitchell says.

"She's not using her car," I say. "I didn't mean to say 'old car.' It just came to me, which means—"

"It's the truth." Mitchell groans. He calls the station again. "Wallace, Skylar Harris isn't driving her BMW. She's in an old car. I don't know what kind or even the color. I know it's not much. Do what you can." He ends the call and huffs. "We're here."

After Mitchell parks the car, we hurry to the front door.

"What are you guys doing here?" Tess asks when she answers the door.

"We need to talk to you about your sister," Mitchell says. "Do you know where she is?"

"Yeah, she just got home a few minutes ago."

We're too late. She dumped the car with Ruben already. I reach for Mitchell's hand and squeeze it. "I need to speak with her," I say. I'll read her. I'll get the information we need out of her one way or another. And I'm not leaving here until I do.

"Come in," Tessa says.

We step inside. Dad and Mitchell are flanking me, and I get the feeling it's to keep me from lashing out at Skylar. I don't blame them. I'm channeling her rage big time right now.

"Skylar, get down here."

"What, Tessa? I told you I have a headache and need to lie down." Skylar's voice comes down the stairs.

"I'm afraid your nap will need to wait," I say. "We just had an interesting conversation with Natalie Courtwright."

Skylar scoffs. "Nothing about Natalie Courtwright is interesting."

"Really? Because she told us how you tried to pay her to change Valentina's routine on beam so Tessa could beat her."

"What? Skylar, what is this about? You don't think I could win on my own?"

"I didn't give Natalie any money. She's lying if she told you I did."

"She didn't say you did. She told us the plan you came up with and how you promised to pay her to switch Valentina's routine, but you decided kidnapping Valentina was a better way to go."

"Kidnapping?" Tessa sounds horrified. "Where is Valentina? Is she okay?"

"Ask your sister," I say. "I know you put Tessa in a trunk and passed the car off to Ruben Ballock. We're going to find her."

"You think you know a lot of things, don't you?" Skylar says, not seeming the least bit intimidated by us.

"How about I tell you a little story," I say. "Stop me if I miss anything."

"This should be interesting." I wouldn't doubt she rolls her eyes when she says that.

"You told us you believed Isabelle got what she deserved, and at the time, I thought you meant all her trophies and medals. But you actually meant her death. You cleverly told the truth but made us think you were talking about Isabelle's wins."

Skylar stays silent.

"I also know that seven years ago, you went hunting with your dad. You're not big on hunting, though, are you? That's why you're not a good shot. But that day, you were by the highway, and you saw Isabelle's car, didn't you? You recognized it. I'm still not sure how."

"Valentina drives that car now. It's a really gross lime green color. Isabelle loved that color, even though it's so obnoxious." Tessa's voice gets really quiet at the end. I can tell she's believing every word I say.

Old car.

Oh my goodness! "You kidnapped Valentina in her own car. Isabelle's car."

"Skylar, tell me you didn't do this," Tessa says.

"Shut up, Tess," Skylar says.

"You took your father's hunting rifle and tried to shoot Isabelle's car, but you shot the truck driver's windshield instead."

"I would have hit her, but she changed lanes. Perfect little Isabelle everyone adored didn't use a turn signal either. I wound up hitting the truck's windshield, and the driver swerved right into Isabelle's car. I guess it worked out better for me in the end anyway."

"I think I'm going to be sick," Tessa says.

"Tessa, come here," Dad tells her. He must not trust Skylar not to use her little sister as a human shield to make a getaway.

"Skylar, Mom was driving behind Isabelle. What if you hit her?" Tessa's in tears now, her sobs choking her voice.

The truth hits me. "You didn't care. You're your father's daughter. But the money, that's your mom's. If she died in that accident, you would've had her money and not had to deal with her being so overprotective anymore. Isn't that right?" I ask.

"Not a bad deal, right?" Skylar's tone holds no remorse.

Deal. That reminds me. "Your family paid Brian Clark, the lawyer representing the truck driver from the car crash. They paid Brian to convince Chad Hooper to settle. Your dad knows. He knows you shot his gun and caused the crash. That's why you two were long gone when the police showed up at the scene. Your father got you out of there and covered it up."

"Except he thought the gun went off by accident," Skylar says.

I have no doubt that's true. He thought he was protecting his daughter, who simply shot the gun by mistake. I'm not sure I can blame him too much for that.

"Why did you go after Valentina? She's my friend," Tessa cries.

"Tess, you're an idiot. You don't make friends with your competition. And Valentina was no smarter. She told you about the routine change. Told you she was going to insist on doing Isabelle's routine instead. I couldn't let that happen."

"When did she tell you that, Tessa?" I ask.

"Yesterday after practice."

"I overheard the whole conversation. I called Natalie, but she assured me she had things under control. I didn't believe her. She wants everyone to think she's so tough, but I know the DiMarcos. You can't change their minds once they're made up. Valentina wasn't going to listen to Natalie. I had to take care of things myself. For Tessa. One of the Harris sisters has to win over the DiMarcos once and for all."

"It's not a victory when you cheat," I say.

She laughs. "Sure it is. Tessa didn't do anything wrong. She won't be penalized for any of this because she didn't even know what was going on. It wouldn't be fair to disqualify her. And now she's going to win. Which means I win. I beat Isabelle once and for all. The DiMarco legend will be erased, and it will become the Harris legend instead."

"You just called me an idiot, and now you're saying you did this for me? What is wrong with you, Skylar?" Tessa is falling apart now.

I hate to say it, but Skylar is showing signs of being a sociopath. She has no remorse for her actions. Even watching her little sister fall apart right now doesn't seem to be having any effect on her at all.

"What's wrong with me? With *me*? I spent years living in Isabelle DiMarco's shadow. No matter how hard I trained, I was never good enough to beat her. She lived in the gym. It was her entire life. It should have been my life. My victories."

"She beat you fair and square," Tessa says. "I don't care when Valentina beats me. She deserves it. And if I beat her, she congratulates me. That's what real competitors do."

"No, you two are jokes. You can't be friends with your competition. Valentina was using you. Pretending to be nice to you. I know because her sister did it to me."

"What are you talking about?" Tessa asks. "You and Isabelle weren't friends.

"You were too young to remember."

"I was ten. I remember just fine. Isabelle was nice to everyone."

"Fake nice. She pretended to your face. Then she'd study our performances and perfect our moves. It was like a slap in the face."

"Did she steal your routines?" Tessa asks.

"Not entirely."

"But we all do the same things. What you're really saying is she was better at it than you, and that made you angry."

"The day I came in second to her, her routine was so similar to mine. You can't tell me she didn't copy me."

"I saw the videos of that competition. Your routines were similar, yes, but she had much more complicated moves in hers. That's why she won."

"She didn't win. I won. I killed her with that trophy that is rightfully mine! And then I got rid of your competition for you, you ungrateful little—"

Tessa screams, and there's a scramble.

"Get off of me! This is police brutality," Skylar yells.

"Skylar Harris, you're under arrest for the murder of Isabelle DiMarco and the kidnapping of Valentina DiMarco." Mitchell reads her rights.

"Can you call one of your parents?" Dad asks Tessa. "I think they need to come home."

Mitchell calls Officer Gilbert to come get Skylar and bring her to the station. He and I aren't finished with this case yet. There's still one more thing we need to do. We need to find Valentina.

"Where did you put Valentina?" I ask Skylar.

She laughs. "I'm done talking to you people."

"Fine. Don't talk." I reach for her, but Mitchell pulls me back. "What are you doing? I need to read her. I can find out where Valentina is."

"Piper, she's completely unhinged. I don't trust her not to headbutt you, kick you, or bite you if you go anywhere near her right now."

"She's handcuffed. You can restrain her."

"Do you want me to lose my badge? We're pushing the boundaries a little too far here. We both know you don't want me on suspension for another two weeks."

Officer Gilbert arrives. "I'll take her from here."

I let out a deep breath. "Did you tell Wallace to look out for Valentina's car?" I ask.

"Yes, I have every available officer on it," Officer Gilbert says. "We'll find her."

Skylar cackles. "You'll never find her. Not in time at

least. That idiot Ballock has no idea there's a girl in the trunk of that car. Valentina is in her final resting place."

"Get her out of here," Mitchell says.

"Mitchell, we have to make her talk," I say.

He grabs my shoulders. "This is a game to her. She doesn't care that we caught her. Her end result is getting Tessa to win on Saturday. With Valentina gone, that's exactly what's going to happen."

No, what's going to happen is Tessa will win, and Valentina will die just like her sister.

CHAPTER TWENTY-ONE

We're going to lose daylight very soon, which isn't going to help the search for Valentina at all. Everyone will be in the dark, just like I am now. Mitchell and I are sitting in his patrol car, debating our next move.

"Do you want to try reading Valentina's necklace again?" Mitchell asks me.

Valentina.

"Yes, I know. I'm not an idiot. I know we need to find her." I grip my hair in frustration.

"I'm not calling you an idiot, Piper. We'll figure this out together," Mitchell says.

"No, I wasn't talking to you. It's my stupid senses. They said Valentina's name."

Valentina.

"Why don't you yell it a little louder?" I say. My goodness. At this rate, I'll be committed for yelling at the voices in my head. I really will need to see a shrink. Maybe Skylar and I will end up in the same psychiatric facility, her being treated for being a sociopath and me for being certifiably insane.

"Piper, I just thought of something."

"What?" I ask, on the verge of tears.

"What if your blindness never had anything to do with Isabelle DiMarco?"

"Of course, it does, Mitchell. I became blind from reading Isabelle's medal."

"I know, but what if you became blind because Valentina can't see right now. What if she's blindfolded, and you need to use your other senses to find her because she can't access her vision?"

Yes.

I swallow hard. "I can't believe this, but you're right. My senses are saying that's what I need to do. I need Valentina's necklace again. I have to sense where she is now." I've done this before when kidnapping victims were blindfolded. In fact, I did it on the very first case I ever worked with Mitchell. That's probably what gave him this idea.

He places his hand on my leg. "Take your time."

"Valentina doesn't have time."

"You can't rush yourself, Piper. You have to tune in to everything. Every sound. Every smell. Everything you possibly can."

"I know." I take several deep breaths. "I'm ready." I hold out my hand to Mitchell, and he places the necklace on my palm.

Darkness.

Chirping birds.

Strawberries.

Sugar.

Freshly cut grass.

I lean my head back on the head rest. "I don't know what to make of this. Maybe she's on a farm or something."

"A farm?"

"I smelled cut grass."

"That could be anywhere, Piper."

"There were birds."

"Again, that could be anywhere."

"Mitchell, that's not helping."

"Sorry. Keep going. Maybe we need to piece all the things together for them to make sense."

"Strawberries."

"There's a strawberry field on the outskirts of town. Maybe that's it."

"Maybe."

"No confirmation from your senses?"

"No." I lower my head and uncross my ankles. My feet hit something. "What's that?" I ask.

"Oh, that's the bag from our donuts."

Maybe that's why I smelled sugar. It was the

powdered sugar on the donuts. I'm sure some is on the bag. "I need to try again."

"Are you sure?"

"I have to. Besides, I haven't gotten a single headache since I lost my eyesight."

"Okay. Here." He touches the necklace to the back of my hand, and I turn my hand over to take it.

I focus on Valentina. I need to hear what she hears.

Darkness.

Chirping birds.

Strawberries.

Sugar.

Freshly cut grass.

"Mmm."

"Jelly donuts," I say.

"They're gone. That bag is empty, and this isn't really the time for one of your donut cravings," Mitchell says.

"No, that's not what I mean. Valentina is somewhere near jelly donuts. I can smell them near her."

"Are you sure it's not that bag that you're smelling?"

"Valentina is smelling it. Not me. And I think Ruben is eating one. I heard him say, 'Mmm.'"

"He stopped for donuts?" Mitchell asks.

"I think so. He's used to living in the outdoors. He probably hasn't had a donut in years. I'll bet he was driving to wherever he's dropping the car, smelled the donut place, and went in for a snack."

"Because he has no idea there's a girl in the trunk. He thinks he's only dumping a car, and there's no rush," Mitchell says. "But which donut place is it?"

That I don't know. "It's not Marcia's Nook. We know that." You can't smell one pastry from another there. This is a full-on donut shop.

"Maybe a chain that's open late?" Mitchell asks.

"No. If you're going to eat junk food for the first time in years, you want the ultimate junk food. I think Ruben went to that homemade donut place near the highway."

"That would make sense because he's probably taking the highway to wherever he's dumping the car." Mitchell gets on his phone. "Wallace, I need a roadblock. Ruben Ballock is going to try to take the highway out of Weltunkin. He's at the homemade donut shop now. Piper and I are on our way there." Mitchell ends the call and throws on the siren.

Since Dad went back to the station with Officer Gilbert and Skylar Harris to help with the police report and give them all the details of what Skylar confessed, it's up to Mitchell and me to catch up with Ruben Ballock.

"The donut shop is set right off of a family farm. It's family owned and operated, according to the big sign," Mitchell says.

That explains the freshly cut grass I smelled.

"And there's the lime green car," Mitchell says. "With Ruben spread out on the hood to look up at the stars."

I squeeze the necklace in my right hand and smile. We made it. Valentina is going to be okay. Tears fill my eyes, and I blink them away. But what happens next makes me cry harder. "Mitchell." I grab his arm.

"What is it?" He parks the car and turns to me. "Did you have another vision?"

"More like I have my vision. I can see." I look into his green eyes and smile.

"I really want to kiss you and celebrate right now, but—"

"We have a teenage girl to save. Let's go." I open my door, loving that I don't need someone to help me out of the car. I walk toward Valentina's old car. Ruben has no idea we're here since Mitchell cut the siren before pulling in.

"Ruben Ballock," Mitchell yells. He has to say it three times before Ruben hears us, but Valentina hears us immediately. She starts pounding on the trunk.

"What's going on?" Ruben asks, climbing down from the top of the car.

"Give me the car keys, now!" I yell.

"You're those people who came out to see me at my campsite," Ruben says.

"That's right, and if you don't give me the keys right this second, I will take them from you and place you under arrest," Mitchell says.

Ruben reaches into his pocket for the keys and then tosses them to Mitchell, who turns and throws them to me.

I unlock the trunk. Valentina is crying and reaching out to me. I remove her blindfold. "It's okay. We're here to save you. You're going to be all right." I help her sit up and get out of the trunk.

"What?" Ruben's face is pure shock. "How did she get in there? I swear I didn't do that to her."

"We know," I say. "Skylar Harris did this. She paid you to get rid of the car, right?"

Ruben nods. "I was going to take it to a junk yard to be compacted."

Valentina sobs harder and leans against me. My senses must be back to normal because I'm instantly overwhelmed by her fear and pain. "Mitchell, help," I say.

He comes over and wraps his arm around Valentina. "Let's get you out of this." He removes the tape from her wrists. "Mr. Ballock, you need to come down to the station with us and give a statement."

Officer Wallace and Officer Lewalski arrive on the scene.

"Valentina, we're going to have your parents meet us at the station. We have a few questions for you, and then you'll be able to go home," Officer Wallace tells her.

"You don't have to be scared anymore," I say. "Skylar's been arrested. She confessed to your sister's murder and your kidnapping. It's all over."

"Hey, you can see again," Valentina says.

"Yeah, it turns out losing my vision was more about

helping you than Isabelle. Or maybe Isabelle was intervening so I'd be able to help you."

Valentina lowers her head, looking ashamed. "I never wanted any of this. I was only doing it for Isabelle."

"I know. And I think Isabelle will be okay with it if you decide gymnastics isn't for you anymore."

"She's dead. You can't possibly know that."

"I know she loved you, despite the fights you two got in. She wanted what she thought was best for you, but the truth is only you know what that is."

"I'm going to do her routine on Saturday. Win or lose. I'm going to do it for her, and then I'm going to hang up my leotard for good."

I nod.

"Will you come to the meet? I think both Tessa and I would like to have you there."

Mitchell comes over and wraps his arm around my waist.

"Detective Brennan and I would be honored to come watch your last meet," I say.

"Yes, we would," he says. "We'll be your cheering section."

"Detective Brennan has been looking for an excuse to break out his pompoms."

Valentina laughs, which was my intention. "Do you really have pompoms?"

"For you, I'll make sure I do."

———

Mitchell and I attend the gymnastics meet on Saturday. We both came equipped with pompoms and two bouquets of flowers, one for Valentina and one for Tessa. In a way, they both lost their sisters in the past few days.

"I can't believe we solved this case in four days. That has to be a record," Mitchell says as we stand off to the side near the Extreme Gymnastics team. Valentina took first place on the beam, and Tessa placed second. They're both standing on the podium, looking happy for each other. How is it that these two sisters could understand the nature of the sport and get along when their older sisters couldn't?

Phoebe Billings will never return to gymnastics after her assault charges. And Natalie Courtwright is retiring from coaching as well. I think Rebel and Extreme Gymnastics will both be better for it. The two gyms will still probably be rivals, but I don't see them hating each other anymore. Hopefully, they all learned something from this.

Ruben Ballock felt awful for his part in the kidnapping. He's being charged with trying to dispose of a stolen car, but he won't face kidnapping charges on top of that. And now that the truth about Isabelle's accident came out, Ruben has been cleared of the previous charges as well. Skylar Harris will spend life in prison for her crimes, but she's also going to get psychiatric treatment, which I really think she needs. I recommended counseling for the entire Harris family and DiMarco family. I think it would help them to talk through their feelings and everything they've lost in the past week. Detective O'Reilly backed me up on that suggestion, and I made sure Chief Johansen knew that I felt Detective O'Reilly needs to get back to field work, even if it's slowly easing her in. Mitchell is still giving her the cold shoulder, but he'll get past this. He has to, because while Detective O'Reilly and I have our differences, I'm not going to let them stop either one of us from doing our jobs.

After the awards are finished, Mitchell and I approach Valentina and Tessa to give them their flowers.

"Thank you for coming," Valentina says. "I still don't know how I pulled off that routine."

"You did it because you're an amazing gymnast, and you had your sister watching over you," Tessa says. "I couldn't be happier for you." She hugs Valentina.

"Yeah, well, the next meet is all about you. I'll help in any way I can," Valentina tells her. "I think I might like coaching better than competing anyway."

"Are you going to coach at Rebel?" I ask her.

"No, I'm taking Paige's former position at Extreme. Paige is now the head coach."

"And I'm leaving Rebel to join Extreme," Tessa says. "I need a fresh start with a new gym."

"I guess it all worked out in the end then," Mitchell says.

"Congratulations to you both," I say.

Mitchell and I walk out.

"One of these times, I'd like to have a happy ending that doesn't come after a death," I tell him.

He rubs my lower back as we walk to my car. I finally got it from the parking lot in front of my office, and I even drove to the meet today. "The bright side is we prevented Valentina's death."

He's right. She would have been crushed to death if Ruben brought the car to that junkyard. I can't even think about that.

"I'm ready to go home and curl up on the couch with you."

"While reading a book?" he asks, slipping his arms around my waist.

"Maybe." I admit there's a flirtatious tone in my voice.

"You look both happy and sad right now. I can't figure it out," he says.

"I'm going to miss the way my abilities stepped up for me when I couldn't see, but I am so thankful to have my vision back." I stare into his greener than green eyes.

"Be honest. When you kissed me when you didn't have your eyesight, did you pretend I was someone else?"

I shake my head. "No. There's no one else I want to be with. Ever." I reach up on my toes and kiss him.

———

If you enjoyed the book, please consider leaving a review. And look for *A Mental Picture Paints a Thousand Crimes* coming soon!

Stay up-to-date on all of Kelly's releases by subscribing to her newsletter: https://bit.ly/2ISdgCU

ALSO BY USA TODAY BESTSELLING
AUTHOR KELLY HASHWAY

Piper Ashwell Psychic P.I. Series

A Sight For Psychic Eyes

A Vision A Day Keeps the Killer Away

Read Between the Crimes

Drastic Crimes Call for Drastic Insights

You Can't Judge a Crime by its Aura

Fortune Favors the Felon

Murder is a Premonition Best Served Cold

It's Beginning to Look a Lot Like Murder

Good Visions Make Good Cases (Novella collection)

A Jailbird in the Vision Is Worth Two In The Prison

Great Crimes Read Alike

I Spy With My Psychic Eye Someone Dead

A Vision in Time Saves Nine

Never Smite the Psychic That Reads You

There's No Crime Like the Prescient

Fight Fire With Foresight

*Something Old, Something New, Something Foretold, Corpse
So Blue*

Murder is in the Eye of the Beholder

Between A Vision and A Hard Case

Madison Kramer Mystery Series

Manuscripts and Murder

Sequels and Serial Killers

Fiction and Felonies

Cup of Jo

Coffee and Crime

Macchiatos and Murder

Cappuccinos and Corpses

Frappes and Fatalities

Lattes and Lynching

Glaces and Graves

Espresso and Evidence

Americanos and Assault

Doppios and Death

Ristretto and Revenge

Traumatic Temp Agency

Corpse at the Candy Shop

Holidays Can Be Murder

Valentine Victim

Paranormal Books:

Touch of Death (Touch of Death #1)

Stalked by Death (Touch of Death #2)

Face of Death (Touch of Death #3)

The Monster Within (The Monster Within #1)

The Darkness Within (The Monster Within #2)

Unseen Evil (Unseen Evil #1)

Evil Unleashed (Unseen Evil #2)

Into the Fire (Into the Fire #1)

Out of the Ashes (Into the Fire #2)

Up in Flames (Into the Fire #3)

Dark Destiny

Fading Into the Shadows

The Day I Died

Replica

ACKNOWLEDGMENTS

As usual, I have to thank my amazing editor, Patricia Bradley, first. Thank you for all the work you put into making these books the best they can be. To my incredible cover designer, Ali Winters at Red Umbrella Graphic Designs, I can't tell you what it means to me that you've put so much effort into the covers for this series. Thank you so much for everything you do.

To my family and friends, thank you for your constant support. To my VIP reader group and my ARC team, you guys are amazing. Thank you for helping me spread the word about this series. And finally, thank you to my readers for spending time with my characters.

ABOUT THE AUTHOR

Kelly Hashway fully admits to being one of the most accident-prone people on the planet, but luckily, she gets to write about female sleuths who are much more coordinated than she is. Maybe it was growing up watching *Murder, She Wrote* that instilled a love of mystery, but she spends her days writing cozy mysteries. Kelly's also a sucker for first love, which is why she writes romance under the pen name Ashelyn Drake. When she's not writing, Kelly works as an editor and also as Mom, which she believes is a job title that deserves to be capitalized.

 facebook.com/KellyHashwayCozyMysteryAuthor

 twitter.com/kellyhashway

 instagram.com/khashway

 bookbub.com/authors/kelly-hashway

CPSIA information can be obtained
at www.ICGtesting.com
Printed in the USA
LVHW112006140622
721260LV00013B/186/J